Return to Lonesome

After Jim Starret was framed for a robbery he didn't commit, he decided it was time to learn how to shoot . . . and when he got out of jail, he went looking for the robber who had caused all his woes.

But Starret's problems were far from over when he gained his freedom. Somebody from his past still wanted him dead. . . .

Return to Lonesome

Brendan Fagan

A Black Horse Western

ROBERT HALE · LONDON

ISBN 978-0-7090-8948-3

Robert Hale Limited
Clerkenwell House
Clerkenwell Green
London EC1R 0HT

www.halebooks.com

Typeset by
Derek Doyle & Associates, Shaw Heath
Printed and bound in Great Britain by
CPI Antony Rowe, Chippenham and Eastbourne

ONE

'You've bin a model prisoner,' the governor said to Jim Starret. 'You've bin granted a reduction in yer sentence fer savin' my life an' fer keepin' some of the other prisoners under control until the army got here to restore order.'

Starret didn't say anything. He was too busy making his own plans.

'I hope yer goin' to leave that business in Lonesome behind you an' git a fresh start some place else.'

'I sure intend to make a fresh start some place else,' Starret heard himself saying to the governor.

'Good fer you,' the governor said, holding his hand out. Starret shook it.

'Thanks fer yer advice,' Starret replied.

Starret walked across the office and opened the door at the far end that would lead him to where one of the trustees was waiting. He handed Starret the brown paper parcel holding the things that Starret had come to the pen with.

The trustee was a small man called Mitch, who had been in the pen for a long time. 'I'm glad yer gettin' out, Jim. That Dawlish, he got himself a reprieve an' they ain't gonna hang him. He said he was gonna git you fer wreckin' his escape plans.'

Starret said, 'Thanks Mitch. I won't fergit the warnin'.' He took the parcel and walked across the room and out of the door into a room where he could get changed.

It was a struggle getting into the shirt. He had put some muscles on when he was breaking rocks in the quarry. When he was finished he went out through the door at the end of the room and to where the head warder and some of the other warders were waiting to sign his release form.

'Hope we won't be seein' you back here,' one of them called out as the outside gate swung open.

Starret walked out into the fresh air and headed for the trail.

He had only gone a few yards when a voice called out. 'Hi, Jim.'

Starret looked at the speaker. 'Frank Rawlins,' he called back.

'Glad to see they kept their word an' let you out early,' Frank Rawlins said.

'I was surprised too. I didn't think the governor would go ahead with it.'

'You still aimin' to do what you said you would do when you were back there?' Rawlins tossed a backward glance at the pen.

'Yeah. Especially since Drake and Piggott won't be gettin' out,' Starret said.

'I've got a horse fer you,' Rawlins said.

'An' a six-gun,' Starret said. 'An' a holster an' ammunition.'

Rawlins led Starret off the trail.

There were two horses in a clearing and Starret saw that one of them had a rig with a six-gun in the holster draped across the saddle.

Rawlins took it down and handed it to Starret, who fastened it on.

'Tie it a mite lower,' Rawlins said, after Starret had got it fastened on. 'It can make a difference.'

Starret adjusted the rig.

'That's fine,' Rawlins said. 'Now git in the saddle.'

They rode for the rest of the day, resting their horses by the trail when they needed a break.

Night found them outside a small town. 'It looks a good place to stay. There's bound to be a boarding house hereabouts,' Rawlins said.

They found one pretty well straight off. After they registered for the night, Rawlins said, 'I feel myself in need of a drink. I think I'll mosey down to the saloon fer one. Comin', Jim?'

'Sure. It seems to have bin a long day,' Starret replied.

'The first day out of the pen usually is,' Rawlins said, going to the door.

They walked down the dark street in the direction of the saloon.

'Sounds a lively enough place,' Rawlins said, pushing his way through the batwings into the smoky saloon.

The place was pretty crowded.

'Beer,' Rawlins said to the barkeep.

The barkeep was a fat, bewhiskered *hombre*. He filled up two glasses and set them down in front of Rawlins and Starret.

'Pretty loud in here,' Rawlins said, after he had paid for the beers.

'There's a couple of hundred beeves on the other side of town. The crew is in here,' the barkeep said. 'They're headin' up to Dodge.'

He turned to serve one of the crew.

The noise grew until Starret could make out the beginnings of an argument.

One of the crew who had been arguing barged into Rawlins, spilling his beer.

'Look what yer doin',' he hollered at Rawlins.

'Sorry, *amigo*,' Rawlins said wiping the beer off his shirt.

The cowboy backed off and the argument started all over again. A minute later he cannoned into Rawlins again.

The cowpoke turned round, his face red with

anger and 'I told you once, fella,' he said.

'Take it outside,' the barkeep told them.

'Like hell,' the cowpoke snarled drunkenly at him.

The saloon had fallen silent as the cowpoke backed away from Rawlins, his hand moving to his gun.

'Let it go, Barratt,' a voice called from the back of the crowd.

'No,' Barratt said, not taking his eyes off Rawlins.

'Yeah,' Rawlins said. 'Leave it.'

'Yer yella,' Barratt said, slurring his words.

'Back off, Jim. Whatever happens, you stay out of it,' Rawlins said to Starret.

The cowpoke's hand dropped to his iron. Rawlins's dropped faster.

The sound of the shot broke the silence in the saloon. Barratt went down.

The batwing doors were pushed open and a *hombre* wearing a star on his chest and carrying a shotgun came into the saloon.

'Drop it,' he said to Rawlins. Rawlins dropped his six-gun.

'Barratt drew first,' a man said, stepping up to the bar.

The sheriff looked at Starret.

'It was like they said. This fella drew first,' Starret said.

'That makes it unanimous. OK, you two,' the sheriff said to Starret and Rawlins. 'Make that the first and last gunfight you have in my town. Ride out at first light and stay out.' The sheriff turned and walked out of the saloon.

A *hombre* came out of the back of the crowd of cowboys. He signalled the barkeep over and ordered two beers. The barkeep put them down in front of Rawlins and Starret.

'I'm Matt Reilly. My herd's at the other side of town, You two fellas have left me short-handed.' He let it lie for minute 'Either of you two boys done any trail drivin' before?'

'I've done it a couple of times,' Rawlins said.

Reilly looked at Starret. 'You?'

Starret shook his head.

'You're a mite young,' Reilly said. 'I heard what the sheriff said. When you ride out, ride close by my herd. Stop by if you want a job.'

Rawlins looked at Starret. 'OK, we'll be there.'

Just after first light Starret and Rawlins headed up to Reilly's herd.

'Glad to see you boys,' Relly said jovially. 'Yer ridin' drag.'

'You'll hate it,' Rawlins told him. 'All the trail dust you can eat.'

They started out shortly after dawn.

It was damned hard work. Ornery beeves and ornery horses. A couple of days out a flash flood swept Sarret off his saddle. Rawlins and Reilly saved him from drowning.

Whenever they got spare time Rawlins took him away from the herd and taught him to shoot.

The trail drive went on until they were within a couple of days of Dodge. The night had come and Starret and Rawlins were out guarding the herd.

'Hear that?' Starret asked Rawlins.

'Yeah,' Rawlins said.

A spatter of gunfire broke the night air.

'Let's git,' Rawlins said, drawing his six-gun, rowelling his horse hard and heading in the direction of the gunfire.

Starret saw them coming out of the dark, flashes of light as the rustlers fired at the cowpokes. He felt something pluck at his hat and reckoned it must be a piece of lead. A rider galloped past him, firing as he went. Up ahead of Starret, Rawlins was heading into three or four of the rustlers. One of them fired at Starret. Then Rawlins's horse went out from under him. Starret tried hard to see where Rawlins was, but a heap of dust was hiding him. Another rustler was riding straight at Starret. Before he could think, everything that Rawlins had taught Starret took over and he shot the rustler out of his saddle.

After that it got confusing and the herd started to stampede. It took the cowpokes the rest of the night and the following morning to get them rounded up and settled down.

Starret found the place where he had last seen Rawlins. There were a couple of the hands stood

11

round talking. They stopped talking when they saw him coming.

'I knew you an' him were buddies,' Reilly said. 'It's a damn shame. We'd have bin in Dodge in a couple days. Did he have any kin?'

'No,' Starret told him. 'He had no kin.'

'OK. You've worked damned hard, an' we're going to show a good profit on this herd, so I'll give you his money. Where did you two meet up?' Reilly asked him.

'The pen,' Starret told him. He could see the surprise in Reilly's face.

The following day Starret started for Lonesome. The day after that it started to rain.

TWO

It had rained solid for most of the day. His hat was plastered to his head, his boots leaked, and the flesh of his fingers was cold and wrinkled as they held the leathers.

The only thing about him that was dry was the low-tied gun, protected by the slicker. Now it was night and he still had a piece to go.

A sudden gust of cold wind blew a hole in the rain, and he saw the light ahead.

'Praise the Lord,' Starret said cynically.

When he got to the house, he dismounted and tied his horse to the hitch rail. It was a relief to be out of the continuous pounding of the rain even though the veranda had more holes in it than a colander.

Taking off his hat, he shook the rain off. He knocked on the door. He took a look round. From what he could see and sense, the place was run down. It was like it was losing the struggle to keep going.

The door opened, and some light spilled out on to the veranda. 'What d'ya want?' the man with the shotgun asked him.

'Somewhere dry an' some hot food. I can pay.' He moved the slicker so that he could get at his money.

'Don't you move,' the old man said. 'Take a step forward so I can see you proper.'

He stepped back to allow the stranger into the house. The door closed quickly with a slam behind him.

'He don't look like one of them, Pa,' the girl said as she came round in front of the stranger.

'No, that's what I was thinkin',' the old man said, less truculently than before. 'It ain't a night for barn burnin'.' He lowered the shotgun.

'Got a name?' the girl asked him.

'Sure,' he said. 'Ain't we all?'

'Yer too wet an' hungry to be sassy,' she told him.

His eyes didn't soften; then he said, 'Jim Starret.'

The girl pushed the pistol into her belt. 'Hand me yer slicker. Then sit down at the table. We got some stew an' coffee left.'

The old man got his slicker from the peg behind the door, and got into it.

'I'll go see to yer horse. Put him in what's left of the barn, an' give him a rub down an' some feed.'

'I'd be obliged if you brought in my rifle. I've got a feelin' that the cover's leakin',' Starret told the old man. He waited until the old man had gone out.

'You an' him got names?'

'I'm Ginny Halton. That's my pa, Silvio.' She filled up his plate with some of the stew from the black pot in front of the fire.

She watched him as he took hold of the eating irons. He ate quickly, tearing chunks off the loaf to mop up the thick, brown gravy.

'You come far?' Ginny asked him when she had poured the coffee.

'A fair ways,' Starret said, in a tone calculated to discourage further questions. He sipped at the steaming coffee as he stared into the fire. The door opened, and he was on his feet, his gun in his hand.

'Take it easy, young fella,' Silvio said in alarm.

'Sorry,' Starret said, releasing the hammer, and dropping the gun into the leather.

Ginny picked up the chair.

'Seems we all got our troubles,' she said.

'Yeah,' Starret told her, and sat down at the table. Ginny and Silvio exchanged glances.

'You're welcome to stay the night,' Silvio said, when Starret had finished eating. 'It's just gonna be a blanket in front of the fire.'

'That would be fine,' Starret said.

'We'll leave you to turn in,' Silvio said, putting a lucifer to a couple of lamps.

Ginny tossed him a blanket.

When they had gone, Starret pulled off his boots, and stretched his legs in front of the fire to dry his

15

socks. After a while he took the cover off his rifle and checked it. When he was satisfied there was no real damage, he unloaded the rifle, checked it and cleaned it.

Outside the wind was rising. The house rattled under the wind.

He woke up suddenly. The wind had dropped to nothing. It had stopped raining. There was only the sound of dripping water as it fell through the holes in the veranda. Then he heard something else. The squelching of boots through the mud, and the jingling of spurs.

Pulling on his boots, Starret drew his .45. There was no time to rouse the others. Whoever was out there was getting closer. Starret reckoned there were three of them outside.

Thumbing back the hammer, he waited. They came crashing into the door, and Starret squeezed the trigger. He heard a scream as the door splintered. A couple of pieces of lead came in through the open doorway.

Starret felt the breeze as they passed his head. Behind him the door of Silvio's room opened, and he felt the hot blast from the shotgun as the buckshot passed over his head. The boom of the gun filled the room.

Ginny came out of her room holding the six-gun she had held on Starret earlier. The gun flamed and Starret heard another scream from the outside. A hunk of lead smashed his .45.

Then it all went quiet. He heard a body being dragged over the boardwalk and, a minute or so later, horses galloping away.

'You OK?' he asked Ginny and Silvio.

'We're OK,' Silvio told him, breaking open the shotgun and pushing fresh loads into it.

'That the way neighbours greet newcomers to this place?' Starret asked them, dropping his damaged .45 into the leather. 'Or are they tired of burn' yer barn?'

Ginny glanced at Silvio. 'It ain't usually that forceful. Usually it's just a burnin' brand or somethin' of that kind. First time it's bin so personal.'

Starret tossed a log on the fire, which had started to burn low, and the morning was still a way off.

'Who are those fellas?' he asked Silvio.

'We ain't rightly sure,' Silvio told him. 'They've bin hittin' places in the valley fer a spell now. Not just us, every place.'

'Ain't the law doin' nothin' about it?' Starret asked him.

No,' Ginny said quickly. 'The law's doin' what he can, but he ain't gettin' any place.'

'Maybe the law's in it with them,' Starret said.

'Jed Fallon, we're startin' to think, ain't up to the job,' Ginny said.

Starret looked at her. She sounded bitter. 'Yeah, it

must be tough,' Starret said.

'Yer welcome here. Sorry about the reception.'

'I don't figure it was yer fault.'

'OK. We'll leave you to turn in,' Silvio said getting to his feet.

'Thanks agin,' Starret said.

Silvio and Ginny went to bed in silence, after they had fixed up the door, leaving Starret to keep the fire company.

THREE

Jim Slocum and Brett Farr were heading up to the cabin in the hills.

They were holding on to Greg Hollister, who had taken some of Silvio's buckshot, and a piece of lead from Starret's .45.

All three were dressed in shabby range clothes, and wore their six-guns tied low.

'How's Greg doin'?' Farr asked Slocum as the three men rode away from Silvio's place.

'Not so great. We're gonna have to stop an' git some help or he's gonna bleed all over the trail from here to hell,' said his comrade, who was holding on to Hollister's arm.

'He's just gonna have to hold on till we git back,' came the impatient answer.

'Slocum, he ain't gonna make it if we don't stop him bleedin',' he was told.

'Then he ain't gonna make it. You just hold on tight

to him. We ain't got that far to go,' Farr snapped.

'There weren't just the two of them in there. There was another fella, him that shot Greg first,' Slocum said, his hand slipping round Hollister's body as the blood seeped through the man's shirt.

The horses were finding the going hard in the clinging mud, and now they were heading up country. The going was getting harder as the horses struggled to get uphill.

Hollister started to moan as the horses turned off the main trail, and approached a cabin, concealed by the thick foliage.

Slocum slid out of the saddle and helped Hollister to the ground.

Hollister screamed as Slocum missed his footing in the mud, and fell.

Farr hitched the horses, and came round to help Slocum. Slocum kicked the door open and struggled into the dark cabin.

'Hold him while I get a lucifer goin' so we can see what we're doin'.'

Slocum dug out a lucifer and scratched it on his belt buckle. The light flared as he lit the lamp.

Hollister's face was pale, and shiny with sweat.

'He's a goner,' Slocum said.

'Better not let him hear you say that,' Farr said with a ghoulish laugh. 'He won't take too kindly to it.'

'Damn right he won't,' groaned Hollister, who had

come round momentarily.

'Sorry about that, Greg, but these wounds are pretty bad,' Farr said as they laid Hollister on the bunk.

'I know it's pretty bad. I can feel it's pretty bad.' Hollister groaned again.

'I'll get a fire goin' an' there's some red eye to ease the pain,' Slocum said, going to the fire.

Farr dug the red eye out of his war bag, and pulled the cork.

Bending, he put it to Hollister's lips. Hollister coughed and choked as some of the red eye went down.

Farr put the bottle to his lips, and took a greedy swallow, then passed it to Slocum. He took a mouthful too.

Ginny fixed up breakfast shortly after dawn. The rain had stopped but it left an empty grey sky that seemed endless. It was quiet in the house as she served up ham and eggs. A couple of times Starret caught her eyeing him curiously.

'Goin' any place?' she asked him.

'Up to Lonesome,' Starret told her, cutting up a slice of the ham.

'Jed Fallon's the sheriff up there,' she said.

'What happened to Dempster?'

'Quit four or five years back,' Ginny said. 'You know him?' She watched him to gauge his reaction.

Starret stayed expressionless. 'I knew him,' he said in the same tone of voice he had used the night before.

'You've got a tight mouth on you,' Silvio told him.

'Got it in pen.'

Silvio and his daughter looked surprised.

'I drew a five-stretch with two other fellas. I came here to do somethin' about it.'

'Like what?' Silvio asked him.

'Like somethin',' Starret said.

Nobody said anything else until Starret was ready to leave.

Silvio saddled up his horse for him, and brought it round to the front of the house.

'How much do I owe you?' Starret asked him when he had got in the saddle.

'Not a dime,' Silvio answered.

Starret gigged his horse on to the Lonesome trail.

FOUR

The ground was like black treacle as the horse pulled itself through the deep, clinging mud. Starret looked up at the sky a couple of times hoping to see a break in the clouds, and a lightening of the gloom. It was as though it was never going to get light again. Sometimes the wind rose, half-dragging Starret's hat off his head.

Lonesome came up out of the gloom, an untidy gaggle of buildings, still wet from the previous day's rain.

Starret saw the sign that said LIVERY, Al Hopkins, Prop. . . .

Dismounting, he banged hard on the door. He pulled down his hat as the wind pawed at it. The door opened, gouging out a furrow in the mud.

'Git in here, an' be mighty quick about it.' The voice was impatient.

Starret pulled on the reins, and the horse followed

him in. The door was pushed closed. Behind him, Starret could hear Al Hopkins wheezing.

Al staggered round to where Starret could see him. He was a small bent man with no thatch on the roof. He was holding a gaudy red handkerchief to his face.

'What'dya want?' he croaked.

'I want you to take care of my horse,' Starret said. 'Give him the best. He's a good horse.'

'I like a fella that knows a good horse when he rides one.' Al sneezed and started to cough. 'Anythin' else?'

'I need somewhere to stay. You got a good word for any place?' Starret asked him, taking down his saddle-bag.

Al thought about it. 'Ma Grindles is the best place in Lonesome. Just round the back of my place, and two blocks down. You can't miss it. Mention my name.'

Starret picked up his saddle-bag, and tossed it across his shoulder.

Outside the rain hit him in the face again, and he scowled. He squelched through the mud, until he could get up on the wooden veranda outside the general store.

Starret looked up at the sign. The name was the same as when he had left Lonesome for the pen. He trudged on until he came to the alley where some wooden boards had been laid in the mud. They sank under his weight. It was the same in the next alley with the mud and water slopping up over the wood, and crawling into his boots again. He was starting to get dammed tired of having wet feet. He looked up at the boot maker's sign. He'd come back when they were open. He looked up and down the street. Everywhere was locked up, as if it was a holiday or something.

There wasn't a soul around in the pouring rain.

'What do you want?' the woman asked as she opened the door.

'Some place to stay for a couple of days,' he answered, dropping his saddle-bag on the boardwalk.

The door opened, and he picked up his saddle-bag, and went inside.

It was as gloomy inside as it was outside. A couple of lamps stood on a couple of small tables in the hall, not giving out too much light. The place smelled damp and felt cold.

Starret thought he might have made a mistake.

'There ain't any place better in Lonesome,' she said. 'At least not with the way things are.'

'Al, at the livery sent me. He said you'd give me a room for the night. Maybe longer.'

'Al sent you?' she said. 'I can fix you up with a room. You want some grub?' she asked him.

'Could use some,' he said. 'Last time I ate somethin' hot it was at breakfast, and that seems like a long time ago.'

'This weather does that to a body. C'mon.'

She took one of the lamps from the table, and led him up the narrow stairs.

'Hold this,' she said, handing him the lamp, and feeling for the key in her apron pocket.

The door opened with a rusty creak.

'This is it. You get yerself ready, an' when you come down, I'll have some grub ready fer you.'

She lit the lamp on the table with a lucifer from a box she had in her apron pocket. Taking the lamp off Starret, she went downstairs.

When she had gone, Starret hung his slicker behind the door, and examined his .45. He needed a new one. He took out the loads and put them in his vest pocket. At the bottom of the stairs, a voice said, 'You ready?'

In the kitchen he found Ma Grindles spooning some stew into a deep plate.

'Sit yerself down,' she said, pointing to a chair at the head of a small table.

Starret sat in the chair, and watched her. When she had filled the plate she laid it in front of him. For a few seconds he looked at it.

'Somethin' the matter?' she asked him.

'Reminds me of the stew I ate last night.'

She gave him a quizzical look. 'An' where would that be?'

'The Halton place,' he said, digging in.

He could feel her interest. 'They still out there?'

He spooned some of the stew into his mouth, and looked at her. 'The barn's still there as well.'

Her thin eyebrows went up. 'They're hangin' on longer than anybody figured they would.'

'What kinda trouble they got?' Starret asked her.

'Maybe the kind that ain't got nothin' to do with a stranger.'

'Fine,' he said.

'Coffee?' she asked him, holding the pot at him.

'Sure.'

She poured the coffee, and put the pot on the table. 'What's yer name?'

'Starret,' he said, waiting for the reaction.

'You've changed the hell of a lot,' she said, after a few seconds.

'I figure most folks would say that. How come I don't recognize you?'

'We lived out beyond the Halton place. We didn't get into town all that much. Pa wouldn't even come in for the trial. He figured—' she stopped.

'Like most folks round here, he figured we did it,' he said, sipping at the coffee.

She said nothing, but continued to stare into the flames.

Starret watched her, trying to remember who lived out beyond the Haltons. Then it came to him – the Baxters, a strange family. Never came into town unless they had to.

He yawned. The woman looked up from the fire.

'Why don't you turn in. You can start what you came to do fresh in the mornin'.'

FIVE

'How's he doin'?' Slocum asked Farr. They were still in the cabin.

'Unconscious again. It ain't lookin' too good fer him. We've got to git him a doc from somewhere,' Farr said. 'Can't seem to stop the bleedin'.'

'Seems like we'd be wastin' our time, his time, an' the doc's if we get him up here just in time fer the funeral,' Slocum replied, forking some beans into his mouth.

'What about the boss, can't he do anythin'?' Farr said, taking a look at the bunk that Hollister was lying on, the sweat shining on his forehead, his eyes closed and his face twitching.

'You know what Randall would say. Save everybody some time an' trouble an' put a bullet in him,' Slocum said.

'Guess he would do at that,' Farr said. 'He's a cold-hearted bastard, even for our line of work.'

29

'So what are we gonna do? We can drag a doc up here fer nothin or put a bullet in him. We could collect his money. Randall wouldn't be any the wiser, nor would Hollister,' Slocum said.

'OK. You gonna do it?' Farr asked him.

Slocum looked down at Hollister. 'No. We cut cards, if it comes to it. Seems the fairest way.'

'You don't sound all that convinced,' Farr said, pouring himself some coffee. 'Ain't turnin' yellow on me?'

Slocum looked at Farr. 'No, I ain't turnin' yellow on you.'

'Sounded like it,' Farr said warningly.

'Just give him a day or so, see how he goes on. I'm goin' to see Randall, an' pick up our money. I'll git Hollister's as well. Don't see no point in tellin' Randall what he don't need to know.'

A couple of hours later Slocum hauled up outside the house of Randall's Rolling R spread. Slocum hitched his horse to the rail, and went up the steps, the rain rolling off his slicker. He went inside.

The Rolling R spread was the biggest in the territory, and Randall wanted it to become even bigger.

'What are you doin' here?' he asked from behind his desk when Slocum walked in. 'I told you not to come here unless you had to.'

'It's pay day,' Slocum told him, sitting down in the chair opposite Randall. 'An' I thought you might be interested to hear about what happened last night.'

Randall's thick eyebrows met over his beaky nose. 'How did it go? Any sign of them gettin' out?'

Slocum shook his head. 'They got some help. Some help that put a slug in Greg. He ain't in great shape. Reckon he needs a doc.'

Randall flared up at him. 'What do you mean by that?'

'I mean there was another player in the game. Pretty handy too. Greg's in a bad way. He's gonna bleed to death unless you git somebody up there right quick.'

'OK,' Randall said to him. He opened the drawer, and took out a wad of notes. He tossed them to Slocum who caught them.

'Yeah, that's it,' Slocum said, putting the notes in his jacket pocket.

'Keep an eye on the Halton place. I'll git a doc up there,' Randall said.

The sheriff was a big man wearing a freshly polished star on his chest, a star that shone like a sun. His big dark eyes reminded Starret of the governor of the pen when he had welcomed Starret and the others. He had said, 'You're here because you committed a crime, an' it's my job to see you don't enjoy yer stay.'

The sheriff had something the governor didn't have, a moustache you could hang your hat on.

The sheriff went on writing for a minute or two

before he looked up at Starret.

'What can I do for you?' His voice was unfriendly.

'Can you tell me where I can find Billy Dempster?'

A light of some sort came into the sheriff's eyes.

'What d'you want to know for?' He gave Starret a few seconds then went on, 'You've got pen written all over you.'

'It's a personal matter.'

'You look a mean sorta fella,' the sheriff said. 'I'll give you just one piece of advice and that just once. Get back on yer horse, an' ride back to where you came from or ride off the edge of the world. Either way, git.'

'I came to see Dempster, an' I'll go when I've finished my business.'

The sheriff came round the desk pretty fast for a big man. He took a swing at Starret. Starret caught the arm and twisted it up the man's back. He kicked the back of the sheriff's knee, and the sheriff folded up and went down.

'I ain't got no quarrel with him, at least I don't reckon I have, an' I sure ain't got one with you. I'm gonna let go of yer hand; just get up, an' sit the other side of the desk, OK?'

Fallon rubbed his wrist, and climbed to his feet.

'Now where can I find Billy Dempster?' Starret asked the sheriff when he had got behind his desk.

'He still lives outside town,' Fallon said glowering at Starret. 'Shacked up with a Mex woman called

Carlota. They ain't married nor nothin'. Ride out of town, an' take the trail that leads up past the river, towards the mountains.'

'Thanks, Fallon,' Starret told him. 'I just want a name from him. Me and two others did five years in the pen for somethin' we didn't do.'

Fallon gave him a sour look. 'Billy Dempster had hundreds of fellas in this jail, an' if I had a double eagle for every one of them that said they didn't do it, I'd be able to move out of Lonesome, an' live somewhere decent.'

'You could start by movin' to the Halton place, an' start makin' that decent.'

'What do you mean by that?' Fallon asked him.

'There's bin some barn burnin' an' the other night it got real personal, in a manner of speakin'. Three fellas tried to kill Silvio an' Ginny. Winged one of them pretty bad unless I miss my guess.'

Fallon looked at him. 'I'm just one man.'

'Just try bit harder,' Starret said.

Fallon rose from the desk, his hands gripping the edges, the knuckles showing white.

'What are you sayin'?' Fallon asked him.

'Fergit it,' Starret said. He got up. 'Obliged fer yer directions.'

Outside the rain had eased off to a thin drizzle. He could only see a few folks about as he walked to the livery.

Al was still coughing, and wheezing. 'Mornin,' he

croaked. 'Come fer yer horse?' he asked Starret.

'Sure. I'm gonna take a ride up to see Billy Dempster,' Starret told him.

'Wife said last night who you were. I remember you an' them other two kids,' he stopped and took a long cough.

'No, we weren't no more than kids,' Starret told him.

'Hope you didn't come all this way to get yerself into more trouble,' Al said.

'No, just come up here to straighten a couple of things out. Be back in a couple of hours.' Starret took hold of the reins, swung himself up into the saddle and headed out of town.

'You Carlota?' Starret called from the saddle. when he got to the cabin.

The girl looked up, startled. It had stopped raining completely now and she was hanging some washing on a line. There was a basketful of washing at her feet.

She put her hands to her eyes to see him. '*Sí*, I am Carlota. Who are you?'

'Billy Dempster around?'

'*Sí*, but who are you, *señor*?' she asked again as he got out of the saddle.

'An old friend of Billy's,' Starret lied.

'Oh, a friend of Billy's,' she said. 'He lives here. I will tell him that he has a visitor.' She went towards

34

the door, but Starret got between her and the door.

He raised the latch and went in.

Billy Dempster was sitting smoking an old pipe in front of a fire; a blanket was over his knees. He was staring into the flames.

'Long time no see, Billy,' Starret said.

He was about to repeat the words when Dempster turned round.

'Who are you?' he asked truculently, screwing up his eyes.

Starret took a step nearer. 'Don't you remember me, Billy? I'm a little disappointed.'

The blanket slid off Dempster's legs, as he took the pipe out of his toothless mouth.

'Starret,' he said, sucking in the saliva from his lips back into his mouth.

'You ain't lookin' so good, Billy. The years ain't bin so kind to you.'

Before Dempster could say anything, the door opened, and Carlota came in holding Dempster's old .45.

'Ees everything all right, Billy?' she asked, pointing the shaking gun at Starret.

'You don't need to point that at me,' Starret told her. 'I don't mean Billy no harm. Just called in to reminisce you might say.'

Carlota looked at Billy.

'That's OK, Carlota,' Dempster said, wiping his mouth with his sleeve.

She looked at Starret, then went outside. Starret stood at the door.

'Carlota ain't the nosy sort,' Dempster said. 'If you come to tell me yer innocent. I've heard it all before.'

'Jed Fallon said something like that,' Starret said, stepping closer to the fire.

The air was still cold.

'Fallon's a bully, but it ain't him you come to talk about. Don't know why Randall put him up fer sheriff.'

'I didn't come to talk about Fallon, not by a long ways,' Starret told him.

'Then what do you want to talk about?' Dempster leaned forward and the blanket slid of his legs again. He pulled it back over his legs. He picked up the box of lucifers from the table by the side of the chair.

It took him a while to get the pipe going again, but he did.

'Who gave you my name for the robbery, along with Piggott's and Drake's, because they're lyin' no good pieces of humanity.'

'It wouldn't do any good,' Dempster said. 'He's dead, an' I ain't gonna drag the name of a good man into your mess.' Dempster started to cough.

Starret watched him. Five years before he would have felt some pity for a soul that was coughing like he was going to choke.

'Good man be damned. He got Piggott and Drake killed.' He knew that Dempster hadn't heard him, he

36

was holding his chest, and breathing heavily.

'Whoever he was, his sort should burn in hell.'

Dempster considered it while he got his breath back. 'He was an honest man.'

'Like hell he was honest. Piggott couldn't take the pen. He hanged himself. Drake got himself killed in a prison riot. One of the other prisoners broke his neck while the guards were tryin' to work out what to do.'

'Sorry to hear that,' Dempster said.

'Ain't you gonna point me in the right direction?' Starret asked him.

Dempster started to get angry, and his face reddened. For a while there was only the sound of Dumpster's hard breathing in the cabin.

'You gonna let it lie?' Dempster gasped when he had calmed down a mite.

'No. It ain't only about me. It's about Piggott and Drake. I owe it to them, an' somebody else owes them a damn sight more. We were friends since we were kids. We grew up together, chased girls together. I owe them. If you won't help me, don't get in my way or I'll kill you, Billy Dempster.'

Dempster looked at him, his eyes angry and at the same time sorrowful.

'Yer makin' a mistake, Starret. Fer yer own good let it lie. He still has friends in this town' an' there's still some bad feelin' on account how some folks lost their life savings, an' one of them lost his life.'

'I'll remember that, Dempster. I'm goin' now. If I come back it might be to kill you.'

Dempster coughed and had some trouble breathing. 'I'll be waitin'.'

Starret walked out of the cabin. Carlota stopped what she was doing.

'Es 'e all right?' she asked Starret as he went to his horse.

'Fer now,' Starret said, hauling himself into the saddle. 'I'll tell you if there's gonna be a change.'

Along the trail, he got to thinking. Somebody had set the three of them up. That somebody was now dead, and had been seen as a respectable man in Lonesome, and it was a pretty good chance that he was the one that had taken the money out of the Lonesome Bank.

SIX

He reached Lonesome and hitched his horse outside the Fair Lady Saloon. Starret stopped, scraped the thick mud off his boots on the step and pushed his way in through the batwing doors. There weren't many people in the saloon.

'Beer,' he said, when he got to the bar.

'Beer it is,' the barkeep said, as he took a glass off the shelf.

Starret put the coins on the bar. The barkeep put the glass in front of him. Starret took a drink.

The beer made his mouth feel better after his talk with Dempster. He drank slowly, rolling it around in his mouth to get the last of the taste out.

'Gonna buy me one? I'm old enough to drink now,' the soiled dove said to him.

Starret looked at her. 'Sure why not? Another beer over here.'

The barkeep came across with another beer.

'Seems like it's gonna be another quiet day, Cheryl,' the barkeep said to the soiled dove when he had put the beer on the bar.

It came as a shock Starret to realize that he knew the soiled dove. The last time he had seen her, it had been at his trial sitting next to her pa. A sweet thing of sixteen. Two years younger than him. Just one of the crowd of kids that he had hung out with. Cheryl Jessup had been the daughter of Lonesome's schoolteacher. Born and brought up in Lonesome, she had moved East with her pa, so he could get a real education and help the kids of Lonesome.

'Didn't recognize you at first,' he said. 'It's bin a long time.'

'Nearly five and a half years,' she said. They didn't say anything for a minute.

'How's yer pa? Still teaching school?' Starret asked, taking another pull at the beer.

'Died of pneumonia in that bad winter a couple of years back.'

Starret swallowed hard. He had liked her old man. He had a genuine fondness for the kids he taught, and he loved teaching. There was nothing he could say.

'I felt that way. It was the same when Ma followed him a year back,' she said finishing the beer.

He watched her brace herself.

'You want to come upstairs? You're gonna have to pay same as the others though. Harold, the fella that runs this place, he's a real stingy bastard.'

The word shook Starret. He had never heard Cheryl swear before. Then he thought that a lot of things must have changed over the years in Lonesome.

Later he walked back towards Ma Grindles. The rain had started again and his boots still leaked.

Starret came to the gun shop. Inside, a lamp had been lit, and he could see a fella hunched over, working on a gun. Starret squinted, as the rain came pounding down beating a tattoo on his back, and weighing the brim of his hat down. Starret looked up at the sign. 'FRED DURKIN', the painted sign across the window said. Starret looked again, and squinted. Sure enough it was Fred Durkin. The last time he had seen him, Fred had been bumming drinks outside the Fair Lady.

Durkin looked up suddenly, as though he realized he was being watched. Starret felt the cold water in his boots. Wiping his eyes, he walked into the shop. The bell over the door gave a tinny sound.

Durkin squinted at him, and put the tool on the workbench. He pushed the gun he had been working on out of the way.

'What can I do fer you?' he asked, wiping his hands on his trousers, and came over to Starret.

'Got a gun?' Starret asked him, taking off his hat. Water dripped off him and formed a small pool by the counter.

41

'Got one I repaired yesterday,' Durkin told him, leaning against the counter. He went through the curtain to the back.

'You got a customer?' his wife asked him.

'Some fella just walked in off the street. He wants a new .45,' he said, picking up the new pistol from the bench.

His wife got up from the chair, and went to the curtain. Her thin fingers opened it a mite and she looked at Starret who was examining his hat. Durkin was running a duster over the gun to put a shine on it.

'You know who you got out there?' she asked him.

Durkin looked at her and got up. 'No, I don't know who's out there,' he snapped. 'I told you he was just some fella that came in off the street lookin' fer a new .45'

'He ain't just some fella. It's Starret.'

Durkin's face paled. He pulled her away from the curtain and looked at Starret.

'It's him,' he said quietly.

Starret had sat in the chair by the counter and was examining his boots.

'Wonder why he came back here?' she asked nervously.

Durkin said nothing, but pushed her out of the way.

'What's got into you?' she demanded, shocked by the push.

'Nothin', he hissed. 'Nothin'. Now hand me that gun. I don't want him in the shop any longer than I have to.'

She picked up the gun and thrust it into his hands.

Durkin ran his sleeve over the gun and went through to where Starred was sitting.

Starret took the gun off him, and examined it.

'A fine new .45,' he said.

'Yeah,' Durkin said.

Pulling out his damaged .45, Starred dropped it into Durkin's hand.

Durkin watched him. 'Good feel to it. Want to try it?'

'No. It'll be fine,' Starret said. He saw the curtain move.

Durkin gave him the price.

Starret peeled off the bills, and put them on the counter.

'Wouldn't like to do me a favour?' Starret said.

'Depends,' Durkin replied.

'Do what you want with my old gun,' Starret said.

'Sure,' Durkin said.

When he got outside, Starret turned and looked through the window.

The curtain had opened and a woman had come from behind it. She was talking heatedly to Durkin.

When he got to Ma Grindles, Starret let himself in with the key she had given him.

'Get anywhere?' she asked him.

43

'Billy Dempster has sure aged. Got a surprise as well, an' guess who served me in the gun shop?'

Ma Grindles poured him a cup of coffee. 'Fred Durkin. I can see why you're surprised.'

'Fred Durkin was bummin' drinks off anybody who would give him the time of day. Now he's runnin' a shop. Can't think how he got the money together.'

'Git himself a wife.' She stared, fidgeting with her spoon.

'Who'd take him on?' Starret asked her, watching her.

'Rebecca Stone,' Ma Grindles said, putting another spoon of sugar in her coffee. 'Jasper Stone's girl.'

'Jasper Stone's daughter?'

'We all figured that Jasper paid Fred to take Rebecca off his hands. Didn't seem like anybody else wanted her.'

Starret looked surprised. He remembered Rebecca Stone from school. A thin awkward girl with a venomous turn of phrase.

'Seems like Lonesome's gonna be full of surprises,' he said softly, almost to himself.

'You're beginning to learn that, Starret,' she said, continuing to stir her coffee. 'Like I've bin thinkin', what good is it gonna do anybody if you do clear yer name? No good will come of it, Starret. It never does.'

*

44

Durkin watched Starret disappear into the darkness.

'Jed Fallon ought to run that fella out of town,' Rebecca Durkin said acidly when she came back into the shop.

Durkin glanced across at her, a look of fear in his eyes. 'Yeah,' he said, his hand trembling. He took the leather apron off. 'I'm goin' out.'

'I hope you ain't started drinkin' again,' his wife said, her voice edged with a warning.

'Just goin' across to see Fletcher. Wasn't lookin' so good when I last saw him.'

'Where was that, down at the Fair Lady?' she rasped at him.

Durkin hung his leather apron and picked up his coat.

It was only early evening when he got outside but already it was dark. He crossed the street, sinking ankle-deep in the mud.

Mounting the boardwalk on the other side of the street, he scraped the mud off the bottom of his boots, and started down the street to a house that stood a little way back from the rest. He could see a light occasionally through the blustering gusts of wind.

Durkin knocked twice before Fletcher opened the door.

'You want to come in?' Fletcher asked him.

'Sure I want to come in,' Durkin said.

Abe Fletcher stepped to one side as Durkin came

into the house.

'Look like you've seen a ghost,' Fletcher said.

Durkin took off his hat and overcoat, and hung them on the stand.

Fletcher pointed Durkin through to the front room. It was gloomy, with only one light standing on the table under the window.

'I *have* seen a ghost,' Durkin said.

'I was jokin',' Fletcher told him.

'I wasn't,' Durkin said, taking the makings out of his pocket and starting to roll a stogie.

'What's that supposed to mean?' Fletcher asked in a puzzled way.

'Starret's in town,' Durkin said, putting a lucifer to his stogie.

'Starret?' Fletcher said, as if he didn't understand.

'Yeah, Starret, one of the fellas that did five years in the pen fer what us an' somebody else did.' Durkin had crushed the stogie out.

Fletcher said nothing; he just stood looking into the fire. 'Do you think he knows?'

'Don't think so,' Durkin said, putting his back to the fire.

'What are we gonna do?' Fletcher said, his voice shaking. He started to tremble.

Randall sat behind his desk in the ranch house looking a mite worried. Something had gone wrong at the Haltons' place and he didn't figure that his boys were being straight with him. Maybe it was time to get Clanton in on this.

An hour later he was walking over to his stables. He had told one of hands to saddle his horse. He swung into the saddle and headed for Lonesome. He rode down the deserted main street. He followed it down to a house at the end.

Getting out of the saddle, Randall looked round. He squelched up the path and knocked on the door. It seemed like an age before he heard the tread on the other side of the door. The door opened.

'What do you want, Randall?' the man with the walnut-like face asked him.

'I got some sick critters,' he said.

The man stepped back. 'And you want some medicine for them?'

Randall stepped into the house. 'Sure, an' it's got to be something strong. I don't see them gettin' any better.'

He followed the man into the living-room, wrinkling his nose as he went.

The room was dark and smelled like a pigsty. One small lamp stood on a table. Randall tried hard to make out the furniture.

'Still ain't yer favourite place,' the man said. Randall could feel the smile on his lips.

'Just tell me how much it'll be an' when can you do it?' Randall said, trying not to gag on the smell.

'How many sick animals?'

'Three,' Randall told him. 'One of them might be dead when you git there, but I still want the other two puttin' down.'

Harry Clanton looked at Randall. 'I'll get up there just as soon as the weather settles down. The price is $500 a head.' He saw the look of resentment in Randall's eyes.

'You got a deal,' Randall replied.

Clanton went to the front window, rubbed his sleeve along it. 'You're in luck,' he told Randall. 'The weather's clearin'. I'll give you a chance to git clear then I can take a ride up there.'

'Thanks,' Randall said and turned to the door.

'The money,' Clanton said.

'Yeah. I almost forgot,' Randall said, taking the envelope from his inside pocket. He handed the contents to Clanton.

'I'll trust you,' Clanton said.

When Randall had gone Clanton went into the kitchen and took a couple of bottles from the cupboard. After reading the labels he put them into a small black bag under the table. Then he went upstairs and took a Navy Colt from the wardrobe and put it in the black bag. It was his insurance in case they wouldn't drink the red eye.

Downstairs he looked through the window. A clear blue streak was showing through the heavy banks of grey clouds. He grinned to himself and poured a shot of red eye into a glass and tossed it down in one.

It warmed his belly. For a while he watched the blue patch grow.

Clanton went out to the back to saddle his horse. He led it round to the front and hitched it to the rail, then went back to get his bag.

'Mornin', Doc,' a woman's voice greeted him as he was getting into the saddle.

'Good mornin', Cheryl,' he called out in reply to the soiled dove's greeting.

'Goin' to see a patient?' she asked.

'Got a sick fella over at Randall's place.' Clanton was in a hurry to get going, but he didn't want to make the girl suspicious.

'Be seein' you,' Cheryl called back as Clanton got into the saddle.

She watched him head down the street. Usually he spent a couple of minutes talking to her, his eyes all over her. Doc Clanton, she thought, looked at her like all the other men did, but he never came into the saloon.

The doc was heading up to the cabin where the three men were. Hollister had been quiet for a spell. Slocum went over to look at him a couple of times.

'He still with us?' Farr asked him.

Slocum looked at him. 'Yeah, but not by much.'

A splashing outside the cabin made him hurry to the window, his .45 in his hand.

'It's OK. It's the doc,' he said, as he watched Clanton climb out of the saddle.

49

Slocum went to the door to let him in.

'How is he?' Clanton asked, as he pulled off his slicker.

'He ain't so great,' Slocum said, dropping his gun back into the leather. 'Surprised he's still with us.'

Clanton went over to look at Hollister. He didn't have to examine him to see that he was almost too late. A little while longer and he could save himself a bullet or a dose of what he had in his bag.

'Ain't you gonna look at him?' Farr asked Clanton.

'Sure I'm gonna take a look at him,' Clanton snarled at Farr. He bent over to look at the wounds. After a few minutes he looked up.

'Is he gonna make it?' Slocum asked him, fidgeting with a deck of cards.

'He'll make it,' Clanton said. 'He's lost a lot of blood.'

'We can see that,' Slocum said.

'Take it easy,' Clanton told him. He put his hand in his bag and took out the bottle of red eye. He handed it to Slocum. 'Git yerselves a drink, fellers.'

Farr looked round for some mugs. He found them on the table where him and Slocum had been playing cards. He filled out two mugs and turned to Clanton, who shook his head. Clanton walked round to the other side of the bunk that Hollister was lying on so that he could watch the other two.

They drank the red eye and Farr filled up the mugs again. Slocum had gone to sit on his bunk.

Clanton watched Slocum's face for signs that the poison was working.

'Sure feel funny,' Slocum said after a few minutes.

'What's ailin' you?' Farr asked him, standing up from the table, the cards spilling from his hands.

'You bastard,' Farr hollered, reaching for his six-gun. 'What have you put in here?' He tried to throw the mug at Clanton. Clanton moved aside as Farr keeled over and fell to the floor.

Slocum sprawled across the table. Clanton checked them. Once he was sure they were dead, he went across to Hollister. He took the pillow from under Hollister's head and pressed it over his face. Hollister struggled briefly, then went limp.

Clanton checked the three men over. Satisfied, he removed everything from the cabin that might have pointed the law in his direction.

He put his slicker on and rode back to Lonesome.

Cheryl was having a slow day. Hardly a man had come into the saloon to buy a drink and no one had come in to pay for her services.

'Don't look like any young fella's gonna come lookin' fer yer services,' Harold said in the afternoon. 'You might as well take the rest of he day off. If anybody comes in, I'll pass him to Sheila.' He nodded in the direction of the girl sitting on a barstool.

Cheryl gave him a look.

'It ain't my fault it ain't stopped rainin' all summer,' he said, glowering down at her.

'Sure, Harold,' she said quietly. Cheryl picked her things up from the room behind the bar and walked out of the saloon.

The rain hit her like a slap. Cheryl braced herself and headed for her home. On the way down the street she saw Clanton riding back to his place.

He looked damn funny, she thought. Like he was a little drunk. He stopped outside his house, dismounted and led his horse round to the stable at the back. Cheryl watched him and carried on to her house.

Clanton hung his slicker behind the door when he got in then wiped his face with a towel. Going into the living-room he poured himself a shot of red eye and swallowed it down in one. For a while he rested in front of the fire he had just banked up, then took a small notebook from his desk and opened it up. In it was listed the jobs he had done for his 'clients' in and around Lonesome. He wrote $1,500 against Randall's name. This done he allowed himself another shot of red eye.

Starret walked down the street towards Fletcher's house, the wind pulling at him as he went. There was a light on in Fletcher's living-room. He knocked once and waited. The door opened.

'Hi, Fletcher,' Starret said over the howling wind.

Fletcher looked at him and looked as if he was going to shut the door.

'What do you want?' he asked Starret.

'Some shelter from this rain while we talk.'

'We've got nothin' to talk about,' Fletcher said, making to close the door, again.

Starret pushed his way in. 'We got a hell of a lot talk about,' he snarled at Fletcher. They were in the hall. Starret grabbed Fletcher by the shoulders and pushed him into the living-room.

'You can't do that,' Fletcher bleated.

'I can an' I have,' Starret replied. 'You're like Billy Dempster. The years ain't bin so good to you.' He looked at Fletcher, who was shaking all over.

'You bin to see Billy?' Fletcher asked Starret.

'Sure. We had a little talk about that robbery.'

'I had nothin' to do with it,' Fletcher said, collapsing into a chair.

Starret looked him over again. 'How come you knew I was back?'

'Some feller told me,' Fletcher said.

Starret said nothing for a while. 'That feller wouldn't happen to own a gun shop?'

Fletcher didn't reply.

'Don't be coy,' Starret said grabbing him by his shirtfront. 'It was Durkin.'

'OK. It was Durkin.'

'So how come you got so close. I can remember the time when you wouldn't spit at each other.'

'Somethin' happened to change that,' Fletcher said.

'Yeah,' Starret said. 'You an' Durkin got together somehow an' pulled that robbery at the bank an' threw the blame on me an' the others.'

'That's a damn lie.' Fletcher pushed himself up from the chair. 'That's a damn lie,' he repeated.

'I ain't figured it all out yet, but when I do I'll be comin' back fer you an' Durkin,' Starret said angrily.

The rain had stopped when he got outside. Starret looked across the street. The gun shop was dark and locked up.

A shot took a chip out of the wood above his head. Starret dropped instinctively to the muddy ground. A second shot took out some more wood. Across the street in the alley next to Durkin's place, he saw a movement. Starret jumped to his feet and ducked into the alley next to Fletcher's.

He fumbled with the slicker trying to get it clear of his gun. A third shot bit into the wood. Starret saw the flash coming from inside the alley. He sent a piece of lead that way. He thought he heard it ricochet off something in the alley.

Starret waited for a minute then feeling that the gunman had taken to his heels, he stood up.

'Hold it there, Starret,' Fallon shouted as he got to his feet. The lawman was standing a few yards away, his gun in his hand, his hat pulled down over his head.

'Glad you could make it,' Starret said, putting his gun away.

'What the hell's goin' on?' Fallon demanded of Starret.

'Somebody tried to put a piece of lead into me,' Starret told him.

'I don't see anybody,' Fallon said.

Starret gave the lawman a hard look. 'With you comin' chargin' down here like a herd of buffalo, he ain't likely to stick around to be introduced.'

Fallon glared at him and looked as though he was going to slug Starret.

'Just where is he?' Fallon bawled at Starret.

'Right across here,' Starret said pointing across the street.

'Let's go see,' Fallon said, starting to walk across the muddy street.

Fallon hesitated at the entrance of the alley.

'You see anythin'?' Starret asked him.

'Did you expect me to?' Fallon asked him. Starret looked at the shop behind him. Durkin's gun shop.

'Maybe he ducked in here,' Starret said to Fallon, indicating the gun shop.

'It won't be him, I saw him on my way down here. He couldn't have got back in time.'

They walked warily down the alley until they got to the end. They came out of it and into the street, which was deserted.

'No sign of anybody,' Fallon said dropping his six-gun back in the leather.

'You expect there to be?' Starret asked him angrily.

Fallon did not reply. 'Keep that gun in the leather,' Fallon told him and walked away.

Starret walked back to Ma Grindle's.

SEVEN

'I'll send a couple of hands to clean the place up. Git rid of the bodies,' Randall told Clanton.

Clanton grunted and finished his drink.

'Might have some more work fer you comin' up shortly,' Randall said.

'Be pleased to take yer money,' Clanton replied, pouring out two more drinks.

They talked for a while, then Randall said 'I'll git back to the ranch an' get my boys to get out there an' get rid of them bodies.'

A while later, Silvio and Ginny rode into town and hauled up outside the sheriff's office.

Fallon came in from the back where the cells were.

'Mornin' Silvio, Ginny,' he said. 'Take a seat.'

'We ain't here to be friendly,' Silvio told him sourly. 'We got hit again. Ain't you gonna do anythin' about it?'

'I'm doin' all I can,' Fallon told him. 'I just can't git a handle on them.'

'Maybe we should think about doin' somethin' about it ourselves,' Ginny flared up angrily.

'I don't want any of that vigilante talk in this office,' Fallon snapped at her.

'Then do somethin' about it,' Silvio said in a milder tone of voice.

'It's OK you talkin' like that,' Fallon said, 'but I can't just do as I please.'

'Fine,' Ginny snapped. 'But do somethin'.'

'I'll take a ride out to yer place,' Fallon said. 'I might be able to pick somethin' up out that way.'

'Maybe that fella that came by can help us. He seemed pretty slick with a gun,' suggested Silvio.

Fallon looked at him. 'Who would that be?'

'Goes by the name of Starret,' Silvio told the sheriff.

Fallon nearly exploded. 'That two-bit outlaw. I had him in here. He was lookin' fer Billy Dempster.'

'Did he say why?' Ginny asked him quickly.

'Gave me some story about not commitin' that robbery. But they all say that.'

Ginny looked at Fallon. 'Maybe he didn't. He seemed honest enough when he shot them trail trash up.'

Fallon gave her a hard look. 'Stay clear of him, Ginny.'

'If you can't help us maybe he can.'

Fallon bit his tongue but said nothing.

'We'd best be goin',' Silvio said to Ginny.

Silvio and Ginny went out into the street. 'Were you serious about askin' Starret to help us?' Ginny asked her father.

'Can't think of anythin' else,' Silvio replied. 'Fallon's not even tryin'. We need a man that can handle a gun, like Starret, an' maybe bend a few rules. I don't like it, but we've got to do somethin'.'

'Where do you reckon he is?' Ginny asked her father.

'I reckon we could ask around town. He's got to be somewhere.'

Cheryl Jessup saw them walking down the street. At first she was tempted to dodge into one of the alleys, still feeling ashamed of being a soiled dove in the Fair Lady, but Ginny saw her and waved to her. Cheryl felt herself curl up inside.

'Hi, Ginny,' she said.

Ginny looked at her and felt a tinge of sympathy for the girl. 'Starret's back in town. We were wonderin' if you'd seen him.'

'I've seen him,' Cheryl said blushing. 'He came into the saloon.' She stopped suddenly.

The Haltons waited in the awkward silence.

'Any idea where he is?' Ginny asked her quickly.

'He's stayin' at Ma Grindle's place fer the time bein',' Cheryl said, her mouth dry.

'We'll take a look and see if he's there,' Ginny said,

sensing her school friend's embarrassment.

'Damn shame about that girl,' Silvio said when they were out of earshot.

They walked down to Ma Grindles.

'Is Starret here?' Ginny asked Ma Grindles when she answered the door.

Ma Grindles went inside and hollered up the stairs. 'You've got some visitors.'

Ginny and Silvio were waiting when Starret got down.

'I'll leave you to talk. I'll be in the kitchen,' Ma Grindles told them.

'What can I do fer you?' Starret asked them when she had gone.

'We've bin to see Fallon about all this trouble we've bin gettin',' Silvio told him.

'An' you got nowhere,' Starret told them.

Neither of them looked surprised.

'Would you help us out?' Silvio asked him.

Starret was quiet for a minute. Then he said, 'Sure I'll help you.'

Silvio looked at Starret. 'If you've been in the pen for five years how come yer so good with a gun?'

Starret thought about it for a minute. 'While I was in the pen, I saved the governor's life during a riot. They let me out a year early on account of that.'

Silvio nodded thoughtfully. 'An' they taught you how to use a six-gun?'

Starret smiled. 'A feller I was in the pen with. He

showed me.'

'You figured it would be useful if you came back here,' Silvio said.

'I got to admit I had that in mind,' Starret told him.

Silvio said nothing for a minute. 'I can't say Fallon's too happy about this, but we've given him every chance.'

'You just let folks know about this, so there's no more misunderstandings,' Starret told them.

It was just getting dark and the rain was still falling when Mahon got his boys together.

'Just make sure nobody gits out alive to tell any tales,' he said to Jim Ryan.

'OK,' Ryan replied, putting his slicker on. The two men went out into the yard. The rest of the hands were saddled up and were waiting for them.

'Mark,' Jessie Carson called to her son. 'Get cleaned up fer supper and stay in.'

Mark Carson was on the veranda of the cabin watching the rain in a bored sort of way. His pa was in the shed cleaning the place out. It had turned into a swamp in there. He came out into the yard and walked over to the cabin.

'You git yerself cleaned up like yer mother says.' He stroked his son's head as he went into the cabin.

'That smells good,' he said, as he kissed his wife on the cheek.

'It's what's left of that hog you butchered. It's all but cooked.'

Mark came in from the back yard.

'What is it?' his mother asked him.

'Thought I heard horses comin' down the trail,' Mark said.

Jessie and her husband exchanged worried looks as the horsemen splashed into the yard.

'Get my rifle,' Mike Carson called to Mark as the first pieces of lead bit into the wood.

Mark climbed up on a chair and took his pa's rifle down from the wall.

Mike took the rifle from him. 'Git under the table with yer ma,' his father called out to him.

Mark followed his ma and pressed close to her under the table.

From beneath the table they heard the gunfire getting louder. There was a brief pause, then Mark heard his pa call out in pain.

Mark scrambled his way from under the table, followed a second later by his ma.

Mike was lying on the floor, a dark patch of blood growing in the middle of his chest.

'Pa,' Mark yelled as he ran to see to his father.

As he screamed out, the door of the cabin was kicked open and a stick of dynamite, the fuse burning, was flung into the cabin. A second later the dynamite exploded. The cabin was reduced to a heap of shapeless timber.

Mahon and Ryan were feeling pretty pleased with themselves as they headed back to Randall's ranch.

Randall was sitting at his desk smoking a cigar and filling out another glass of red eye when they got back there.

'It go all right?' he asked Mahon, handing him a glass of red eye.

'Sweet and simple,' Mahon told him with a grin, as he took the glass of red eye and went to stand by the fire. 'They didn't know what hit them.'

'Here's to us,' Randall said, raising his glass.

The following morning Fallon was sitting at his desk when Dave Henley came into his office, his face red with anger. 'It's damn well happened again,' he shouted at Fallon.

'What's happened again?' Fallon asked angrily.

'There's bin another burnin', only this time it looks like they used dynamite.'

'Where?' Fallon asked, coming round his desk.

'The Carson place. It's just bin blown to hell. Them fine folks along with their kid. This time you've got to do somethin' about it.'

'I'm doin' all I can,' Fallon said.

'Then how come you're sittin' in here, instead of gettin' out there an' gettin' them murderin' bastards caught?'

'There ain't gonna be anythin' to see,' Fallon said angrily. 'Nobody's gonna leave a trail in this weather.'

'You're a mess, Fallon. Sooner this town has some decent law the better.'

Fallon subsided into a beaten silence.

'I'm gonna see if I can find somethin',' Henley yelled at the sheriff. Henley stormed out of the office, slamming the door behind him.

He rode hard up to the Carson place. He dropped out of the saddle and walked towards what had been the cabin. Henley walked through the mess taking a look at things. After half an hour he sat on a tree stump, the rain bouncing off his slicker.

'Yer gonna git pneumonia sitting in the rain,' a voice said, suddenly breaking into his train of thought.

He looked up quickly to see Silvio looking down from his saddle.

'Mornin', Ginny, Silvio.' Henley said, getting to his feet.

EIGHT

Silvio and Ginny had come into town after meeting up with Dave Henley.

'Dave Henley's bin to see Fallon. Fallon ain't no use,' Silvio said.

'I figured he wouldn't be,' Starret replied.

'We're gonna be seein' other folks, an' if they agree maybe you could figure all this out.'

'Maybe I could,' Starret said. 'But it ain't why I came here.'

Ginny looked up quickly. 'I don't think these happenings are tied up with what befell you, but you might git to the bottom of that as well.'

'It's a long shot, but you could be right,' Starret said, finishing the coffee.

Silvio got up to go. 'I'll go an' see what the other folks say. Some of them ain't happy with the way Fallon's handlin' things.'

When they had gone Ma Grindles came into the

65

living-room. 'There's somethin' hot in the kitchen. I still say that no good will come of this.'

It took Silvio most of the day to go round the small ranches.

'I got a heap of support,' he told Ginny when he got back to the ranch that evening. 'The pastor's goin' to loan us the church hall so we can have a meetin'.'

'I hope this thing works out,' Ginny said filling out his plate.

'I'll go an' see Starret in the mornin' so he can get down there.'

Starret was leaning against the hitch rail outside the Fair Lady. He had to admit that he was getting nowhere in trying to discover the truth about the robbery. It had seemed like a great idea when he was in the pen, but now in the cold light of day he had to accept that he was baffled.

'You gonna stand there all day?' a voice behind him said suddenly.

'Nice to see you, Cheryl,' he said.

'It's a mite early for many folks to be drinkin' but Harold's cleanin' the place out, so if you want somewhere warm to do yer thinkin' come inside.'

Starret followed her through the batwing doors. Harold was at the far end of the bar sweeping up. He raised his head to look at them. A scowl came across

66

his face when he saw Starret.

'Mind if Starret does some thinkin' in here?' Cheryl asked him.

Harold just nodded then went back to his sweeping. 'If he drinks he pays.'

Starret sat down at a table. Cheryl went upstairs.

'You gettin' anywhere?' he asked Starret sourly when he had finished sweeping the floor.

Starret looked at him in surprise.

'Don't worry,' Harold said to him. 'I don't like you fer what you did. Caused some trouble in Lonesome.'

'We didn't do it,' Starret said to him.

'They all say that,' Harold said. 'I gotta admit it was strange. Durkin, he started soberin' up not long after you went to the pen. Stopped comin' in an' bummin' drinks. Cleaned himself up. Got friendly with Fletcher. Got himself married to that Rebecca Stone.'

Starret looked up at him but didn't say anything. He was quiet for a moment, then, 'Why didn't Billy Dempster say anythin' when I went up to see him?'

'Dempster was a good man. Came as the hell of a shock when he turned his badge in, but we figured it was him gettin' on in years. Maybe he couldn't be bothered. An' it did seem funny you three boys bein' out by the swimmin' hole. I know it was summer but it just didn't seem right.'

'Thought Dempster turned the badge in because

it was gettin' too heavy fer him to carry.'

'Most people thought that way,' Harold said. 'But I think Randall or somebody leaned on him. It was him that put Fallon up fer that badge for all the good it did Lonesome.'

Starret looked up sharply. 'Why would Randall put Fallon up fer the badge?'

'You've sure bin away fer a spell,' Harold said. 'Fallon's related to Randall in some way. Don't know how. I think another thing that got folks so riled up was the fact that none of the money ever turned up. Just disappeared into thin air.'

Starret moved in the chair. Maybe there was some link there, he thought. If Fallon was related to Randall that would be why nothing was being done about all the trouble folks were having.

'Glad to see that somebody's takin' notice,' Harold said rising from the chair.

'Anythin' else?' Starret asked him.

Harold hesitated then said. 'That Carlota that goes up there. She don't do it fer nothin'. Somebody's got to be payin her, an' it ain't Dempster. Got barely enough to buy smokin' tobacco.'

Starret got up from his chair. 'Tell Cheryl I'll see her later.' Starret stopped as he got to the batwings. 'Don't tell her what you've told me.'

'OK,' Harold said.

The trail up to Billy Dempster's cabin was wet and

dreary. A couple of times Starret looked behind him. He felt as if he was being followed.

He knocked hard on the door. It took a while for it to open. Carlota gazed worriedly at him.

'You again?' she said angrily.

'Me again,' Starret told her. 'I want to see Billy.'

Carlota tried to close the door. 'He is too sick,' she said.

Dempster was sitting staring into the fire with a rug over his legs; the fire was crackling. Dempster looked across the small cabin at Starret.

'What d'you want?' he croaked.

'Why did Randall fix it so Fallon could get yer star an' why did you quit?'

There was a noise behind Starret. He turned quickly. Carlota was taking a pistol from the bag on the table beside the door. Starret grabbed the gun and pushed her away.

'Leave her be,' Dempster said, his chest wheezing.

Starret unloaded the .45, dropped the gun to the floor and put the loads in his vest pocket.

'You all right, Carlota?' Billy asked her, pulling himself up in the chair.

'*Sí*, Billy, I am all right.'

'I came here to ask you why Randall put Fallon up fer yer star?' Starret said.

Dempster looked as though he was going to die in his chair. 'I don't know,' he snapped at Starret.

'You know, Billy,' Starret said.

Dempster coughed and wheezed again.

'Come on, Billy. You ain't got long. Die with a clear conscience.'

Dempster cooled down a mite. 'My conscience is a damn sight clearer than yours,' he choked. 'I ain't got a robbery on my conscience.'

Starret bit back at him. 'An' what happened to the money. None of us had a cent on us when you picked us up.'

The three of them were quiet for a while. Then Dempster started to choke again.

Carlota stepped forward and held on to Starret's sleeve 'Go, for the love of God.'

Starret looked at her and then at Billy. 'You're no use to me dead. I think you know a heap more than yer sayin'.' He turned and walked out of the cabin.

Starret rode back to town.

He hitched his horse outside the saloon. Silvio came across the street to speak to him. 'Me an' Ginny got it all set up. The hall is just down the street. Most of the folks who are comin' will be there already. Let's be gettin' down there.'

Starret followed him down the street. At the end he saw Ginny standing outside a new-looking hall.

'Everybody's inside,' she said to Starret.

The place was pretty near full. A couple of the people in there gave Starret a curious look. Ginny led him down the aisle to a raised dais. He followed her up and stood behind a small table.

'I'll do the talkin',' Silvio said to him. He turned to face the audience. 'We all know why we're here,' he started, pointing to Starret.

Somebody at the back cut him off. 'I'm Joe Riordan. An' we all know who he is,' he said, as he stood up and pointed at Starret. 'An' we all know where he should be.'

There was a mixed reception to this.

Silvio go to his feet. 'He's done his time an' we need him. If it wasn't fer him me an' Ginny might not be here now.' The noise quietened down.

Somebody else stood up in front of Riordan. 'I don't know this man. I'm new round here, but I reckon we should give him a chance.'

'Thanks, Longstreet,' Silvio said.

'This is the crook who emptied the bank an' caused us some harm,' Riordan went on.

'That was way back,' Longstreet put in, determined to have his say. 'An' that useless feller that wears the star ain't gettin' the job done.'

Starret took a step forward. 'I can understand yer feelin's, but a couple of my friends died in the pen, so I owe them an' I want to find the man who fingered us for what somebody else did.'

There was a silence as people took in what Starret said.

'If you want Starret to help us, then say so,' Ginny said.

Starret watched the people in the hall.

'OK,' Riordan said. 'But if he makes one mistake, then we'll lynch him.'

'Looks like you're hired,' Silvio said.

At the back of the hall no one noticed Bill Tunstall slip out into the street. He hurried quickly down to Fallon's office.

'You got trouble, Fallon,' he said to the sheriff.

'What d'you mean by that?' Fallon asked him.

'The town hired itself a vigilante. Reckon he's gonna bring these hellraisers in.'

Fallon looked shaken. 'Damn him,' he said.

'What are you goin' to do?' Tunstall asked him.

Fallon looked like he didn't know what to say.

'I guess you got some thinkin' to do,' Tunstall said.

Randall's face became red and twisted with rage when Fallon told him that the town was getting Starret to wipe out the band that was doing all the burning and killings.

'We're gonna have to do somethin' about this *hombre*,' he said to Fallon.

'Tunstall heard them talkin'. Starret's goin' up to the Carson place tomorrow.'

'You don't worry about it. Just leave it to me.'

He watched Fallon ride back to town then got Mahon to saddle up his horse.

Clanton was in when Randall got there.

'You got another little job fer me?' Clanton asked him, pouring two glasses of red eye.

'Sure I've got another little job fer you,' Randall said. 'Starret's gonna be up at the Carson place tomorrow.'

'Same deal as before?' Clanton asked him.

'Sure,' Randall told him. 'Just make sure you do it pretty quick. I think this Starret fella is goin' to cause a heap of trouble if we don't step on him pretty quick. He's goin' up to the Carson place early tomorrow,' he repeated.

'Starret?' Clanton echoed.

'Sure, Starret,' Randall said. 'You know him?'

'Knew a *hombre* of that name in the pen. He did a stupid thing. Saved the governor's life. That's why he got out early.'

'Time you put things straight,' Randall said with a sneer. 'Maybe you could do it for free.'

'An' maybe you could do it yerself, fer free,' Clanton snarled.

They both finished their red eye and then Randall headed back to his ranch.

NINE

'I'm gonna take a ride out to the Carson place,' Starret told Silvio early that morning.

'Do you want me to come with you?' Silvio asked him.

'Thanks, Silvio, but I guess I can manage.'

He rode out of town unaware that Clanton was watching him. Clanton followed him from a safe distance, his rifle covered in the saddle holster.

Starret dismounted when he got there and hitched his horse to a fence.

Clanton stopped a hundred yards back, tied his horse to a tree and crept forward. He checked the rifle.

Starret was standing where the front door had been. Clanton got as close as he could with low shrubs between him and Starret. Slowly, he raised the rifle and aimed at the centre of Starret's back. Starret was still looking at the ground. As Clanton squeezed the trigger, Starret knelt to examine a hoofprint on the ground.

The shot went over his head. Starret threw himself into the ruined cabin, crawling on his belly over the muddy ground.

Clanton fired another shot, but Starret had his handgun out. Clanton moved back to where his horse was hitched as some of Starret's lead came pretty close to where he had been.

Slipping the knot that held his horse, he manoeuvred the animal between himself and Starret. He rode Indian fashion, low over the horse's neck, making it hard for Starret to get a bead on him.

Starret ran into the open and emptied his gun in Clanton's direction.

'Damn,' Starret swore as he put fresh loads into his gun.

He got into his own saddle, but Clanton had too big a start on him and Starret lost him in the rocky country around Lonesome.

'I lost him,' he told Silvio when he got to their place in the evening.

'You didn't get a good look at him?' Silvio asked, filling up a mug of coffee.

'No, I lost him an' it was getting dark.'

Ginny came in. 'I dried your horse off,' she told him. 'Yer more than welcome to stay the night, if you don't mind sleeping in front of the fire.'

'Thanks, but I'll get back to Lonesome to see how things are there,' Starret said.

Silvio saw the look of disappointment in Ginny's face when Starret had gone.

TEN

Randall was damned angry when Clanton came over to his ranch after outrunning Starret.

'I thought I could rely on you,' he said to Clanton, offering him a glass of red eye.

'Just damn bad luck,' Clanton said evenly. 'I'll git him next time.'

'Be sure you do,' Randall said. 'I've got a feelin' this *hombre* could be real dangerous.'

'Don't you worry. He's stayin' at Ma Grindle's. If I have to I can git him there.'

'Just make sure you do,' Randall said.

Clanton said nothing; he just rode back to his place. When he got there he lit a lamp and took out his notebook in which he kept a count of the jobs he had done, for whom and how much he had been paid. He poured himself a couple of shots of red eye and settled down to examine the entries. He knew that Randall wouldn't pay him for today. He only paid by results. Clanton didn't mind. He had a tidy sum in a couple of banks outside Lonesome.

After a couple of drinks he felt the need for some female company. He didn't need a woman often. Just now and then. He could manage without them. He hid the notebook away in a set of drawers upstairs and headed down to the Fair Lady.

Cheryl was in the bar when he got there. She saw him coming and moved down the bar next to Sheila, the other soiled dove.

'Beer,' she heard him say, hoping that he hadn't seen her. Clanton drank slowly from the glass, watching the people in the bar. She watched as he drank his beer and looked at the other soiled dove. At first she thought she was going to be lucky, but she was wrong.

She heard him say to Harold, 'I want that young one. Cheryl, her name is.'

Cheryl felt sick. It was hard enough being a soiled dove, but with some of the men she just felt sick, and Clanton was one of them.

'Will you take him?' she whispered to her friend, Shelia.

'He asked fer you. I've had him once an' I told Harold I'd quit if I had to go with him again. We've all got to do our share an' I think you need bringing down a mite. Just because yer pa was a schoolteacher, doesn't mean you're better than the rest of us,' she said with a sneer.

'Cheryl,' Harold shouted down the bar. 'The gent ain't got all night.'

Cheryl walked slowly to the staircase with Clanton right behind her.

'That wasn't so bad, was it?' Clanton asked her when they had finished.

Cheryl bit her lip and didn't answer him.

'You've got a good one there, Harold,' Clanton said, as he walked out of the saloon.

'I hope you ain't expecting a bonus,' Sheila said.

Starret was walking back from the livery to Ma Grindle's place when he saw a figure coming out of the saloon. It was too dark to see the man's face but Starret felt sure he had seen the way the man walked some place before. He crossed the street and followed him for a spell, listening to him splash through the puddles. He watched as the man let himself into a house off main street. He still hadn't seen his face, but he knew the walk from somewhere. Maybe it was on the way to Dodge where he'd learned to handle a six-gun.

When the door closed Starret went over to Ma Grindle's.

'You don't seem to be getting any place fast,' Ma Grindles said, as she served him up his night meal.

'I went out to the Carson place and some sidewinder took a shot at me,' he said.

'Damn shame,' Ma Grindles replied, filling out a cup of coffee for herself.

Starret ate quickly and hungrily.

'Huntin' bank robbers must give you the hell of an appetite,' she said to him when he had finished.

'So does gettin' shot at,' Starret said, taking a drink from his cup of coffee. 'On the way back here from the livery, I saw a *hombre* comin' out of the Fair Lady. Didn't see his face, but I recognized his walk. He turned off main street, an' went into a house that was set back from the street.'

Ma Grindles looked sharply. 'He's a strange one. Set himself up as doctor a couple of months back. I ain't had much to do with him. I stuck with the old doc who'd bin in town fer years. Died a little while before you got here.'

'What name does this new doc goes by?' Starret asked her.

'Clanton. Ezra Clanton.'

Starret shook his head 'That ain't the name I got in my head,'he said draining his coffee cup.

ELEVEN

Clanton locked the door and went into the living-room. He had seen Starret when he got outside the Fair Lady. It had been hard not to panic when he recognized Starret but he managed to keep a cool head as he walked back to his house. He figured that Starret hadn't recognized him so that would give him some time to work out what to do about him.

He lit a couple of lamps, then banked up the fire and poured himself a shot of red eye. He sipped it while he worked on a plan to fix Starret. He knew where Starret was staying, so maybe one night soon he'd go out with his Bowie knife and cut Starret's throat. The thought gave him some pleasure. He had a couple more shots of red eye before turning in.

Starret rose early and fixed himself a cup of coffee before Ma Grindles was awake. The identity of the man who had come out of the saloon still nagged at him as he moved down the darkened streets towards

Durkin's shop.

Despite the early hour there was a light on in the back. Walking round to the front he looked in through the window. As he got there he saw Rebecca Durkin going into the back of the shop. He wondered where her husband was. She turned and walked quickly through the beaded curtain to the back. Starret waited a minute, opened the door and went inside.

He listened but could hear nothing. He moved quickly across the shop and went though to the back. The woman was standing with her back to him examining a .45.

'Yer husband not in yet?' he asked her quietly. Rebecca Durkin turned quickly, the colour draining from her thin face.

'I don't mean you no harm,' Starret told her.

'What the hell do you want?' she demanded acidly.

'I want to know where you an' yer husband got the money fer this shop? From a bank robbery?'

'No, you got the money from the bank robbery. You an' yer friends. Can't say I'm sorry about what happened to them down there.'

Starret made to grab her by the throat then stopped himself. 'You always knew how to rile a feller,' he told her angrily.

'You an' yer friends asked fer all you got,' she hissed at him.

'We didn't do nothin'. Some other *hombres* did that

robbery. I was wonderin' where you got the money fer this place. Last I saw of yer husband, he was bummin' drinks outside the Fair Lady.'

'That was a long time ago,' she said. 'It ain't no business of yours where the money came from, but if it gets you out of here – my brother struck gold. I'd looked after him when Ma died. It was his way of payin' me back.' She stopped speaking like it was a relief getting it off her chest.

Starret searched her face. It was empty.

Behind him he heard someone coming in through the curtain. He turned to see Durkin standing just inside the doorway.

'What the hell is he doin' here?' Durkin asked in a frightened way.

'Just come to ask yer wife where the money for this place came from,' Starret said coldly.

'An' you got yer answer,' Rebecca put in quickly.

Durkin still looked frightened.

'You got anythin' to add to that?' Starret asked him.

Durkin shook his head.

'I can't say I believe you,' Starret told them. 'So I guess I'll just go on lookin'.'

Starret walked out into a thin drizzle and a weak light.

'Morning,' he said to Al when he went down to the livery to get his horse.

*

Randall rode into Lonesome that afternoon with some money for the bank. 'Good afternoon,' the manager greeted him when he walked in with a thick envelope.

'I want to put this in my account,' Randall said cheerfully, handing over the envelope.

Anderson, the manager, took the envelope. 'You just wait here while I give it to one of my cashiers.' When he had gone out Randall sat in the chair waiting for Anderson to come back.

'Sorry for the delay but one of my cashiers had something to tell me.'

Randall wasn't that interested, but he figured that it might be a good idea to keep in Anderson's good books.

'My head cashier saw that man that robbed this bank a few years back heading up to Billy Dempster's place again yesterday,' Anderson said.

Randall went cold.

'You look surprised,' Anderson said.

'It's just that I don't like the idea of that sidewinder bein' around.'

'I've got to agree with you there,' Anderson said, handing over the receipt.

Randall took the receipt and put it in his billfold. 'I've got to be goin'. Just remembered somethin' back at the ranch. I'll see you later in the week.'

Once he got outside, he took a deep breath and walked round to Clanton's place.

'From the look on yer face I reckon you've got another job fer me,' Clanton said, when they were in the sitting-room of his house.

Randall didn't like the smug tone in Clanton's voice. 'Yeah,' he said.

'You gonna tell me who it is or do I just guess?'

'The old sheriff, Dempster,' Randall said.

A cynical smile came over Clanton's face. 'Dempster. I could be tempted to do it fer free while he was a lawman, but I won't. With him bein' a lawman, or ex-lawman, I ain't an' it's gonna cost you more. Say $500 extra. Dempster's still a popular feller round here.'

Randall thought hard for a moment. '$500 extra it is.'

'Glad you didn't argue or it might have cost you even more. I'm takin' a big risk. Does that Carlota still look after him? The Mex bitch?'

'Yeah, she still goes in every day an' gits him some food from town an' cooks his meals.'

Randall gave Clanton the money and rode back to his ranch.

Clanton put the money away and sat down with a shot of red eye. This one would take some planning.

Walt Myers, Lonesome's head of the council, was speaking to Silvio in the church hall along with the pastor.

'Yeah, I've heard about it, an' I've got to agree with

85

you. Fallon ain't doin' the job.'

'You gonna get him out?' Silvio asked him.

'I guess so, but three other members of the council have got to go along with me.'

'OK,' Silvio said. 'Just do it as quick as you can.'

Myers left them in the saloon and went to see two other members of the council.

'Hi Ben, Silvio Halton's bin round drummin' up support to get rid of Fallon,' Myers said to Ben Brooks.

' 'Bout time somebody did. The fella's about as much use as, damn it, I can't think of anythin', but sure, you got my vote.'

'Thanks,' Myers said, leaning down from the back of his horse to shake Ben Brook's hand.

The next ranch was the smallest around. Billy Briers saw Myers coming from a way off. He went back into the house and strapped on his .45. Billy hadn't much use for a gun, but things were changing.

'Hi, Walt,' he said when he got out on to the veranda.

'I can understand yer feelin's,' Walt said when he reached the ranch house. 'I come across a feller that'll help us.'

Briers looked at him for a moment. 'You mean that Starret that was supposed to have robbed the bank a few years back?'

Walt climbed down and walked on to the veranda.

'What do you mean, "supposed" to have robbed the bank?'

'I don't know fer sure, but it always looked funny to me. How come three young kids could have figured out how to get into a bank like that?'

'Got to admit that thought crossed my mind a couple of times,' Walt replied, thoughtfully.

'Their families were respectable folks. They were only just out of school,' Briers said. 'It ain't like they were in trouble all the time. Not like that bank manager's kid. What was his name Ralph? Yeah, Ralph – one of them fancy back East kinda names.'

'He's still around,' Walt said. 'I think maybe I'll mention it to Starret when I see him agin.'

'As fer him helpin' us, sure count me in,' Briers said.

Later that day in town, Silvio mounted up and headed back to his ranch. Ginny met him coming in.

'You look mighty pleased fer yerself,' she said to her pa.

'We've got to get one more name then Fallon's out of a job.' He laughed. 'Got somethin' else as well. Walt told me that Billy Briers had somethin' to say about that robbery. He ain't sure that Starret an' them other fellers did it.'

'What are you gonna do about it?' she asked her father.

'As soon as Starret gets sworn in, I'm gonna tell him. He'll have a badge so he can try to find out what happened, and clear this mess up as well,' he said.

'I sure hope so,' Ginny replied.

Starret had gone up to Boot Hill to take a look at his parents' grave. The shock of the robbery and the trial had helped put them there and Starret wanted to put things right for them.

He walked back down to Lonesome, his feet sinking into the clinging mud and coming out with a squelching noise. Piggott's pa lived in a cabin a few yards from Boot Hill. Starret rapped hard on the door and waited. After a few minutes he heard Jim Piggott dragging himself to the door. He opened it.

'Jim Starret, I heard you were in town. Thought you'd forgotten me.' His grin was lopsided and it pulled his face out of line. He stepped to one side and gestured for Starret to come in.

Starret sat down in one of the two chairs in front of the fire. There were only two chairs in the house. Old man Piggott's wife used to sit there, but the news of her son's death in prison had hastened her own death.

'Glad you ain't forgotten me,' old man Piggott said, dragging his wasted leg over to the chair that had once been his wife's.

'You don't have to tell me you and my boy didn't do it. None of you could have.' He stopped talking and warmed his hands by the fire.

'Tell me about how my boy died, if you know,' he

said, his mouth sounded dry and like it was all an effort. 'All we got was a letter from the governor saying that he had died, and that was it.'

Starret had thought about it for a while and decided in the end to lie.

'Yer boy had an accident while we were breaking rocks in the quarry.' He hoped it sounded convincing. And it looked like Piggott's old man believed it.

'Was it quick?' Piggott's father asked after a while.

Starret braced himself for it. 'He didn't know a thing about it. Yes, it was quick.' A guard had broken Piggott's neck in a second. He had jumped from behind him during the riot and that had been it.

'I'm glad he didn't suffer,' the old man said.

Starret felt like a heel.

'What are you goin' to do now?'

Starret said straight out, 'I'm gonna stick around Lonesome till I find the feller or fellers that did it.'

Piggott's old man went misty-eyed. 'You were always one of the best round here.'

'I don't know where to start,' Starret said thoughtfully.

'Naw, there ain't many likely folks around,' the old man said. 'Nobody came into a heap of money, except Fred Durkin. An' that might have bin her ol' man's money.'

'Fred Durkin?' Starret asked.

'Rebecca Stone musta talked some sense into

him,' Piggott's father said.

Starret looked at the old man. 'Maybe she did,' Starret said, standing up to go. 'I'll get back an' see you sometime.'

The old man struggled to his feet, and led Starret to the door.

'Thanks fer callin',' he said. 'It's bin nice seein' you. If you feel like talkin' just come an' see me.'

'I wish I could have bin more use to yer boy,' Starret said, heading for the door.

Silvio was waiting in the small ranch house when Starret got there that evening. 'Nice to see you again,' he said when Starret arrived.

'I've bin so see Jack Piggott, you know, Harry's dad.'

'How is he? I keep meanin' to go over an' see him, but the way things are, I just don't get the time.'

'The ol' man ain't lookin' so good. That stroke must have taken the hell of a lot out of him,' Starret said, sitting down at the table.

'I got some news fer you. Walt saw Billy Briers, an' he gave him the name of a feller that might have had somethin' to do with it. Not exactly to do with it, but somebody we all forgot about.'

Silvio stopped speaking and sat down.

'Who would that be?' Starret asked hopefully.

'Ralph Anderson. You remember Ralph Anderson, the manager's boy?'

'Sure I remember him. He was a good few years older than most of us,' Starret replied. 'Always had an edge to him. Were does he hang out now?'

'Got the same job in Fairfax. Ten miles north of here. He got some expensive ways. Likes the tables and the girls,' Silvio told him.

'I'll go up an' see him in the mornin',' Starret said, as Ginny came in with a couple of trays of food.

'You look pretty hungry,' Ginny said in a forceful way, putting the plates down on the table.

'Now I come to think of it, I do feel hungry.'

They ate mostly in silence. She looked away quickly when she caught his eyes on her.

At the end of the meal Silvio got up from the table and pulled his slicker from the peg and put it on.

'I'm gonna check on things outside,' he said and went out into the rain.

'It seems a shame to ride back in the rain,' Ginny said.

'Ma Grindles will be expectin' me,' Starret said in a half-embarrassed way.

'If you ever need a roof over yer head,' Ginny said, 'you're welcome here.'

'I expect I'll be back when I got this business sorted out,' he told her, leaning across the table and putting his hands on hers.

A second later the door burst open and Silvio lurched in, his slicker open down the front and blood coming out of it.

Starret jumped to his feet and caught Silvio. Quickly, he lowered him to the floor.

'One man, outside with a Bowie knife,' Silvio gasped.

'Take care of him. I'm gonna see who's out there,' Sterret called to Ginny.

He opened the door and went outside. He saw a man and turned to face him as a bolt of lightning lit up the sky.

'Dawlish,' he yelled as the man came in his direction, the Bowie knife in his hand.

A bolt of lightning lit the man's face up again.

'Dawlish,' Starret shouted again. His finger curled round the trigger. As he hollered two things happened. Ginny came out of the house, Silvo's .45 in her hand. The bolt of lightning hit the tree and sent a branch in Starret's direction. It hit him on the side of the head and knocked him out. Ginny fired at Dawlish, but he was heading in the direction of his horse.

She stuck the gun in her belt and dragged Starret to his feet as he started to come round. They got inside and she bolted the door.

'How's yer pa?' Starret asked, rubbing the side of his head.

'I think he's OK,' Ginny said.

'I'm all right. It looks worse than it is,' Starret said, pulling off his slicker.

'You know him?' Ginny said. 'Where from?'

'From the pen. He's called Sam Dawlish. I figured they were gonna hang him, but he got a reprieve,' Starret said. 'Used to be a gun fer hire. It was the hell of shock to see him in that rain with that Bowie knife.'

Ginny came over with a damp cloth in one hand and a bottle of red eye in the other. She sponged Silvio's face off and fixed him up with a shot of red eye.

'Ginny, fix Starret up with a blanket and a shot of that red eye,' Silvio said from his chair after Ginny had cleaned him up.

The following morning Starret headed up to Fairfax.

TWELVE

Fairfax was the same size as Lonesome. Starret hitched his horse to the rail and looked up and down the main street. It had stopped raining, but the sky was still full of heavy-looking grey clouds. There was more rain up there, Starret reckoned. He walked down to the bank and went inside.

There were only a couple of tellers in the bank working behind the counter.

Starret went to a pretty young female teller. After a minute she looked up from the pile of notes she was counting.

'Yes, sir?' she asked in a pleasant voice.

'I'd like to see the manager,' he said to her.

'What name is it?' she asked Starret.

Starret thought for a moment then said, 'Just tell him an old friend from Lonesome.'

The girl scurried away and knocked at a door marked 'Manager'. Then she disappeared inside.

She came out a few seconds later and said to Starret, 'Mr Anderson will see you now.'

Starret walked down to the end of the counter where Anderson's office was.

He lifted the bar and went behind the counter. He pushed the door open and went inside. Ralph Anderson was sitting with his head down and looking over some papers. Starret closed the door with a bang. Anderson looked up.

There was no hint of recognition in his face.

'I'm sorry, Miss Lever said you were an old friend from Lonesome.'

'Hi, Ralph. Jim Starret, remember me?' Starret asked quietly.

Anderson's face took on an new expression, surprise then fear.

'Yeah, I know,' Starret said. 'I've changed.'

'What the hell do you want here?' Anderson demanded, trying to keep his voice down.

'I've bin in Lonesome, tryin' to figure who framed us for robbery of yer pa's bank.'

'Go to hell,' Anderson said. 'You an' yer miserable friends pulled that robbery an' you got sent to prison fer it. Damn near killed my pa.'

'Prison sure killed my friends,' Starret said, his anger rising.

'Get out, Starret, or I'll call the sheriff,' Anderson said, rising from the chair.

Starret knew he had handled it all wrong. 'OK. I'll

get out but it won't be fer five years this time.' He turned and walked out of the office.

As he walked down to the front door he could feel the eyes of the tellers on his back.

He reached for the handle to open the door when it burst open in his face.

'Where's that bastard Anderson?' a heavy-set fellow yelled as he pushed Starret out of the way.

Starret walked past him and stood in the street for a minute.

There was a saloon across the street. He crossed over and went inside. There weren't many folks in there. The barkeep looked him up and down.

'Beer,' Starret said when he went to the bar.

The barkeep brought the beer down to him. Starret stood drinking it. Then he heard the batwing doors open. The man that came in was the man he had seen going into the bank. He watched for a few minutes as the barkeep and the man talked together. After a few minutes the barkeep went off to serve another customer. The man Starret had seen going into the bank stayed, nursing his drink.

Starret left him for a couple of minutes. He was sure riled up about something.

Starret sidled up to him. 'Say, you don't seem too happy about somethin'.'

'That damn feller, Anderson. He's got some nerve,' Starret was told. 'Seems to think he can do as he damn well pleases, just because he owns the only bank in Fairfax.'

'That bad is it?' Starret asked him.

'I own the stage line that runs to Lonesome. I'm insured with him. A couple of days back one of my stages got stuck up. They got away with $2,000. He won't pay up an' the law ain't much use. Say, I don't recall seein' you round here before.'

'I've just got into town,' Starret said. 'Where did the stage get stuck up?'

'Out by Boulder Canyon. It's a fair bet the Fentons did it. Anythin' gets stolen round here, it's a fair bet the Fentons had a hand in it. Say, what's yer name?'

Starret hesitated for a couple of seconds. 'Jim Starret.'

The stage owner looked at him for a few seconds. 'Can't say I've heard the name hereabouts. I'm Billy Day.'

'Good to meet you,' Starret said. 'Another drink?'

'Don't see why not,' Day said, signalling the barkeep.

They talked for a while. Then Starret said. 'How much if I git yer money back?'

Day looked at him curiously. 'I'll give you $100. Might throw in another $100 if you bring in the four owlhoots that did it.'

'Got yerself a deal,' Starret said, holding out his hand.

Day's meaty fist closed round Starret's.

Starret was set to walk out of the saloon when Day

called out. 'Do you know where Boulder Canyon is?'

'Sure,' Starret called back.

The Fentons, he thought. Things sure didn't change. Starret walked out of the saloon and crossed the street to where his horse was hitched. He slipped the knot and got into the saddle and pointed his horse in the direction of Boulder Canyon.

It was a half-hour ride to Boulder Canyon. Starret was familiar with the country round there. As a kid he had relations up that way, and he thought maybe there was some of them left. The canyon itself narrowed before opening out at the other end.

The trail was badly rutted, filled with black treacly water. He knew he hadn't a hope of finding any tracks.

Starret rode up to the top of the canyon then rode along the wall. For a moment he was thinking of turning back when something in the grass caught his eye. He hauled on the reins and got down. A blue silk handkerchief lay on the ground. Starret picked it up and examined it. In the corner were the initials R.A.

'Hell's bells,' he said to himself. He wrung the wet handkerchief out and put it in his saddle-bag.

He climbed back into the saddle and looked round. 'It has to be here somewhere,' he said to himself. He rode on until he came to a cabin lying in a fold in the ground. As he got near the door opened and a tall bearded *hombre* came out holding a shotgun.

'Put it down,' Starret said with a laugh. 'You ain't

gonna need it, Billy.'

'Cousin Jimmy,' Billy shouted back. 'I thought you were still in the pen.' He stopped and Starret got out of the saddle.

'Yeah, you thought I was still in the pen.'

Billy looked embarrassed. 'We know you didn't do it,' Billy said, taking the loads out of the shotgun and putting them in his pocket. He put his arm round Starret's shoulder and guided him into the cabin. 'I've got some red eye I'd like to share with you.'

Starret sat at the table while Billy took a bottle of red eye out of a cupboard, put two glasses on the table and sat opposite Starret.

'Was it bad in the pen?' Billy asked in a worried kind of voice.

'No need to be like that,' Starret said to him. 'Yeah, it was bad. Two of my *amigos* got killed while they were in there.'

'But you made it out OK?' Billy asked him.

Starret nodded after he had taken a drink from his glass.

'What do you aim to do now?' Billy asked, taking out the makings and building himself one before handing them to Starret.

Starret started to roll himself a stogie.

Billy put a lucifer to it.

'I aim to git them fellers an' make them pay like we had to pay.'

'Just make sure you get the right feller or you

might be havin' somebody comin' after you.'

'I stopped off at Fairfax before I came up here. I bin talkin' to a feller called Day. Seems he's bin havin' some trouble.'

'Yeah. One of his stages got robbed not long back,' Billy said. 'Got any ideas?'

'Unless things have changed a heap round here, it's probably the Fentons,' Starret said.

Billy thought for a minute. 'You're probably right,' he said.

'I sometimes expected them to come into the pen, but it didn't happen.'

'They were pretty smart,' Billy said.

'An' pretty greedy, as I recall.' Starret finished his stogie.

'You gonna go after them?' Billy asked him.

'I guess so,' Starret replied. 'Anyway, I've got to be gettin' back to town,' he said, getting to his feet.

When Starret got back to town, he hauled up outside a boarding house.

'Just give me a room fer a couple of nights,' he told the attractive young girl on the desk.

She handed him a key and gave him an appreciative look as he went up the stairs.

Starret tossed his saddle-bag on the bed and took out the handkerchief he had found near Boulder Canyon. He looked at it closely. The initials were clear enough and the handkerchief had an expensive feel to it.

Starret looked at the initials for a while, then it came to him. The only *hombre* he knew in Fairfax with those initials was Ralph Anderson.

For a moment he thought about it then he went down to the counter clerk.

There was nobody near the counter when he got there, except the girl.

'Hi, Mr Starret, is yer room all right?' she said with a smile.

'The name's Jim, an' everything's just fine. You don't happen to know anybody with the initials R.A.'

The girl thought hard for a minute then shook her head. 'The only person I know is Ralph Anderson, the bank manager,' she said.

'Thanks,' Starret replied, 'I guess I'll go an' have a bite to eat.' He turned and walked to the door.

'You gonna be in town long, Jim?' the girl asked as he reached the door.

'Can't say fer sure,' he said.

'I'm through by nine o'clock. I could show you around,' she said.

After having something to eat Starret went down to the sheriff's office. The sheriff was a small man with watery eyes.

'Yeah?' he said.

'You got any leads on who pulled Billy Day's stage robbery? If you ain't I'd talk to the Fentons.'

'I ain't an' if I had what's it to you?' the sheriff asked.

'Billy Day offered me $100 to get his money back

an' another $100 to get the fellers that did it,' Starret told the sheriff.

'Damn Billy Day an' damn you, whoever you are,' the sheriff replied. 'An' who told you about the Fentons?'

'It ain't strictly my job to ask the Fentons. It's yours,' Starret snapped at the sheriff.

'Then why do you ask,' the sheriff said getting to his feet.

'I knew a sheriff like you. He weren't much use either,' said Starret.

'Get outta my office, mister, or you'll be spendin' some time in one of my cells.'

'I'm goin',' Starret said and went into the street. He took his horse to the livery to get him watered and fed.

'Does ol' Jake Fenton still live out by Boulder Canyon?' he asked the liveryman as he fed his horse.

The liveryman looked at him in a strange way. 'Sure. You a buddy of his?'

'Not exactly,' Starret said stretching the truth. 'I used to be a buddy of his a while back. I thought I'd look him up while I was in the neighbourhood.'

'Yeah. He's still out there. I'd be careful though. He's still got a wild streak in him. Might just take it into his head to shoot you the minute he sees you.'

'Thanks,' Starret said.

Outside, he mounted up and headed for Boulder Canyon.

It was pretty quiet when he got there. Starret headed to the top of the canyon, then in the direction of the Fenton place. He came to a small hill and got down out of the saddle. He led his horse into the cover of some trees. Starret climbed the small hill and looked down on to the cabin. It seemed quiet enough. He cat-footed down the hill and looked round. As he was looking he heard the jingle of spurs and the sound of men talking behind the cabin. He lifted the latch and the cabin door opened. Starret went inside. The place was untidy. He looked quickly round the room. From what he could see there wasn't anything there to help him. A sudden burst of laughter at the back of the cabin made him cross the room to a door.

Starret went through it and found himself in the only other room in the cabin. Lying on the floor was a bag marked 'Fairfax Bank'. Starret picked it up and pushed it into his gun belt. A piece of sacking covered the front window. He moved quickly to the window and pushed the sacking aside.

He got out quickly Outside it was flat and open. The only shelter was a wooden barn near the corral. His gun in his hand Starret ran that way.

His ears alert for any sound that would tell him he had been seen, Starret went to the barn.

He opened the door a little way and looked inside. He could see no one. Starret wondered how long it would be before someone came into the barn with the horses. Not long, he reckoned before they found him in there. The bag would have to do. He would have to get out of the barn without being seen. He saw old man Fenton coming from behind the cabin and going to the corral leading the horses. The old man unsaddled them, threw the saddles across the rail of the corral and then went back into the cabin.

Starret waited. Slowly, the daylight started to fade. Over his shoulder he could see the light from the cabin. He ran across the open ground to the hill. Throwing the occasional glance over his shoulder he could see that no one had come out of the cabin. From the top of the hill he could see his horse silently waiting for him. Starret half-ran, half-slithered down the hill. He grabbed the reins, put foot in stirrup and hauled himself into the saddle.

Starret spurred his horse and headed for Fairfax.

A light burned in the window of Billy Day's stage-line office. Tethering his horse to the hitch rail, Starret went inside.

Day looked up from his desk. 'You got any good news fer me?'

Starret tossed the bag on his desk. 'Got this fer you,' he said.

Day's eyes lit up. He grabbed the bag. 'Was it the Fentons?'

'Sure it was the Fentons. I didn't git the money though. I reckon you'll have to git a posse up. They might still have the money in there.'

'I'll git over to the sheriff. You wait here till I git back?'

'Tell me in the mornin'. I got to see somebody.'

'Thought you'd forgotten about me,' the girl from the boarding house said.

'Got held up, you might say,' Starret said to the girl. 'Say, what's yer name?'

'Rita,' she said coyly. 'I've bin thinkin' about that handkcrchief. Let me have another look at it.'

Starret handed it to her. Shc looked closely at it.

'R.A.' she said after a moment. 'Yeah. I think it might be his. Yeah, that will belong to Ralph Anderson, the feller that runs the bank down here.'

'He live hereabouts?' Starret asked.

She looked at him. 'Yeah, just on thc edge of town. Why?'

'I think I'd like to take a walk down there an' see him,' Starret said, fingering the butt of his .45.

'I'll come with you,' Rita said.

'There's no need fer that,' Starret replied.

'He's a jumpy kinda man. If you go down there, he might take a shot at you.'

Starret doubted this, but he said, 'OK. You stay out the way if things turn nasty.'

'I'll sure do that,' Rita told him.

They went into the street. Starret followed behind. They passed saloons, the gunshop and the general store until they came of the edge of town.

Rita led him down to the last house just outside town. It had a white picket fence running round it. From what Starret could see it looked pretty well kept and respectable. That didn't cut much ice with him. He had known a couple of respectable criminals while he was in the pen.

As Rita got to the front door, Starret put his hand on the butt of his .45.

The girl knocked twice and stepped away from the door. A few minutes later the door was opened by a tall man dressed in clothes that looked like they'd come from back East.

'Yeah?' he said to Starret.

At that moment Rita pushed Starret in the back and he crashed into Ralph Anderson. Both men fell in a tangle inside the door.

'He found that damned handkerchief near where you an' the Fentons robbed the stage.'

Starret and Anderson managed to untangle themselves and were getting to their feet when Starret heard Rita close the door.

'Leave the gun where it is,' she said to Starret.

Starret turned to see her holding a small calibre pistol on him.

'You an' yer fancy ways. I always said you'd get us hung,' she spat at Anderson.

Her face was a mask of hatred and Starret could see the gun twitching in her hand.

'You stupid bitch,' Anderson yelled at her. 'Why

did you have to bring him here?'

'What else could I do? I think he's already sent a posse out there.' Rita's trembling started to get worse.

'Put that gun down,' Starret said to her. 'It's only robbery. Pull that trigger an' it's gonna be murder.'

'Damn you, Starret. Why didn't you stay in Lonesome where you belong?' she snarled.

'I used to belong in Lonesome, but the pen widens yer horizons,' he said.

Rita was stunned by the way things had turned out. Starret ran at her and grabbed the gun from her. He turned quickly in time to see Ralph Anderson searching for a gun that was inside his jacket. Starret pulled the trigger. The bullet threw Anderson back into the hall, blood appearing on the front of his shirt.

'You've killed him,' Rita screamed. 'The only man I loved.' She threw herself at Starret.

Starret opened his mouth to say something, but the force of Rita's body caused him to pull the trigger. She fell back holding her chest. For a moment Starret stood looking at both of them.

He went outside, having taken the key from Anderson's pocket, and locked the house up. Then he got down to the sheriff's office. At the end of the street he could see a commotion outside it.

Billy Day was just coming out when he got there. Day saw him and came running over a smile on his face. 'Glad you're here. We got three of them an' most of the money.' He shook Starret's hand like he couldn't stop.

'Thanks, Billy,' Starret said.

'Let's git inside, so I can show you what we've got.' He forced his way through the crowd.

'Here's the feller,' Day said to the sheriff. 'He's the one that found these owlhoots.'

The sheriff extended his hand. 'Thanks, Starret,' he said. 'The saloon's gonna be open yet fer a while. I reckon Billy owes you a drink.'

'Before we do that,' Starret said to the sheriff, 'you'd better get down to the Anderson place. There's a couple of bodies that have to be taken care of.'

Day and the sheriff looked at him.

'That Anderson fella was in on this. An' that woman Rita had somethin' to do with it.'

The sheriff and Day exchanged glances. 'OK. I'll take care of it after you've had a drink on Day,' the sheriff said.

'I'd like to talk to them fellers for a minute,' Starret said.

'Can't see it doin' any harm,' the sheriff replied.

He led Starret down a narrow corridor to the cells.

Old man Fenton was sitting on a bench looking pretty miserable. His two boys were standing in the corner, not looking much happier.

'Got a visitor fer you boys,' the sheriff said.

Jake Fenton looked up. His boys glanced at Starret and the sheriff.

'This fella wants to talk to you,' the sheriff said.

Jake Fenton got up slowly from his bunk. 'What's in it fer us?' he asked the sheriff.

'Depends on what you got to say to him,' the sheriff said.

'You be careful, Daddy,' Elmer, the elder boy said.

Both boys came to stand behind their pa.

'Yeah, you git somethin' outta this fer you an' us,' Matthew, the younger boy said quickly.

'Dependin' on what you say to this feller, all I can do is speak to the judge before the trial,' the sheriff told them.

'Looks like we're gonna have to trust him, Daddy.'

'It's about this Ralph Anderson feller,' Starret started by saying.

Jake scoffed. 'Anderson is as big a thief as us,' he said. 'He's bin cookin' the books at his bank fer a while. He owes some money to the gamblin' houses round here. It was his idea to rob Billy Day's stage. He rode out in his fancy clothes an' got changed. Left them in the cabin. When we were plannin' it, we'd had a couple of shots of red eye, an' he can't take drink like me an' the boys. He started braggin' how he'd helped rob his ol' man's bank an' got three young kids sent to the pen fer it.'

'Did he say who else was in on it with him?' Starret asked. Ezra gave a laugh. 'No, by damn. He passed out right after he'd had a drink. When he come round, he said it was true, though.'

'You believed him?' Starret asked him.

'Yeah. He was too yellow to lie. I think he'd bin doin' the same at this bank.'

'You sure?' the sheriff asked him.

'Yeah. He'd bin playin' fast an' loose with one of his young lady tellers as well.'

'Thanks a heap,' Starret said.

'You an' Day get down to that saloon,' the sheriff said.

Day and Starret headed down to the saloon and had a few drinks.

Next day, feeling a heap better about things, Starrett took the trail back to Lonesome.

When he got there he took his horse to the livery.

'Ma Grindles has bin worried about you,' Al said to him. 'She figured you could have come to a bad end.'

Starret walked down to Ma Grindles but met up with Silvio on the way along with a couple of council members.

'We're gonna tell Fallon he's out of a job. You comin' with us?'

'Sure,' Starret replied.

'What do you want?' Fallon asked when Silvio and the others got there.

'We've bin to see the council, Fallon. You're out of a job,' Silvio told him. 'Now hand yer badge to

Starret. He's takin' over from now on.'

'Starret?' Fallon said angrily. 'That two-bit outlaw.'

'Just hand over yer badge,' Silvio said.

Starret picked it up from the desk and pinned it on.

'You got business here?' Silvio asked Fallon.

Fallon stalked out of the office.

'Now you can get on with puttin' these rustlers down,' Silvio said.

Clanton dismounted and walked back down the trail until he could see Billy Dempster's cabin.

He pulled his watch out of his pocket and looked at it. Any time now Carlota would be coming out of the cabin to go into town for Dempster's stuff.

He watched as Carlota came out of the cabin holding a basket. He watched as she rode into town.

Clanton walked towards the cabin, a .45 stuck in his belt.

Dempster was sitting by the fire. At first he didn't hear Clanton when the killer eased the door open.

'Who the hell are you?' Dempster asked when he turned to face Clanton.

'You wouldn't know me,' Clanton said with obvious pleasure in his voice. 'I've come to send you to hell,' he said, taking the .45 from his belt and drawing the hammer back.

'What d'you mean by that?'

'I've come to kill you,' Clanton said.

Dempster coughed and said, 'I ain't afraid of dyin'.'

'Just as well,' Clanton replied coldly and squeezed the trigger.

The bullet slammed into Dempster's chest lifting him out of the chair then dropping him back into it.

Clanton gave a smug look at the body, turned and walked out of the cabin.

Half an hour later Carlota came back, the basket slung over the pommel of her saddle. She got down, hitched the horse to the rail and went into the cabin.

'You asleep, Billy?' she asked, not seeing the blood on his chest.

She started to get the stuff out of the basket and put it on the table.

'Billy,' she said when the basket was nearly empty. When she got no reply again she went across to where Billy was sitting. When she saw the blood she started to scream.

A while later she went outside and mounted her horse again.

'Where's Fallon?' she asked Starret when she got to the office.

'He don't work here any more,' he said. He turned from the board.

She saw the star on his vest. 'You are the new sheriff? No?'

'Yes,' Starret said, 'is somethin' wrong?'

'Billy is dead,' she said to Starret, then started to

cry again.

Starret helped her into a chair. 'Tell me all about it, if you feel up to it.'

'I found him with a bullet in him,' she said between sobs.

Starret looked at her. He had to go up to the cabin, but he didn't want to leave her alone.

'Stay here,' he told her and went down to the Fair Lady.

Harold was in the bar waiting on a few customers. 'Is Cheryl around?' Starret asked him.

'Yeah. She's in the back,' Harold told him.' I'll give her a call.'

'That'd be fine,' Starret said.

'I've got Carlota in my office,' he said. 'Somebody's shot Billy Dempster. Will you stay with her until I git back?'

'Sure,' Cheryl said to him. She collected her cloak from the back and followed him out.

At the office Carlota had calmed down.

'I'll git back as soon as I can,' Starret said and went to get his horse from the hitch rail.

He rode up to the cabin. Hitching his horse to the rail, he drew his .45 and went inside.

Billy Dempster still lay in the chair. The blood on his vest had dried.

'Nothin' to help me,' Starret said after he had looked around.

'Did you see anyone while you were up there?'

113

Starret asked Carlota when he got back to the office.

Carlota shook her head.

'You got any place to stay?' Starret asked her.

'No. No place,' she said.

'Cheryl, can she stay with you fer a while?' Starret asked the soiled dove.

'Sure she can,' Cheryl said.

Starret watched as Cheryl took Carlota to the door. When they had gone he took out his .45 and checked it. He was going down to see Clanton. He walked down the mud-choked street until he came to Clanton's house. From where he was standing on the corner, it didn't look like there was anybody in there. Starret knocked hard, keeping one hand on his gun. As he had half-expected there was no answer. He tried again. No response. Starret looked up and down the street. It was empty. He walked round the back and looked around. There was no horse in the stable.

He looked at the back door then tried it. He pushed against it. It wasn't all that secure. Bracing himself he leaned hard against the door and pushed. It gave.

The inside was pretty untidy. Starret opened the cupboard up and looked inside. There was the usual stuff from the general store.

Starret went through the house and found nothing. The way he figured it, Clanton would be back.

He fixed up the back door so it looked like nobody had been in there.

Silvio was waiting for him in his office. 'Got any ideas who's bin doin' all this burnin'?' he asked Starret.

'The only person that might fit the bill round here is Randall and his Rolling R outfit. The tricky bit is provin' it. Randall has bin buyin' up spreads for next to nothin'. In some cases he's just bin movin' in when them that lived there has moved out.'

'What are you goin' to do about it?' Silvio asked Starret.

'I'm gonna have to catch him red-handed or get one of his boys to squeal.'

'Do you think it will be easy?' Silvio asked him.

'No, I don't figure it will be easy,' Starred replied.

'Have you got any ideas?' Silvio asked him.

'Yes, but folks round here are gonna have to help out,' Starret said, filling the coffee pot that was getting ready to boil.

'They'll help,' Silvio said eagerly.

'Fine. Git everybody together at yer place tonight an' I'll tell you what I have in mind.'

THIRTEEN

That night all the small ranchers met at Silvio's place.

'Glad to see you folks,' Starret said. 'Like I told Silvio, I've got a feelin' that Randall is behind this. We need to catch him red-handed.'

There was a murmur of agreement in the ranch house.

'Have a couple of yer men out at night watching Randall's place, then follow his men when they leave to do the burnin', and git word to me. I'm spendin' some time at Silvio's. Then track his gang back to Randall's place. I'll meet you there an' we can round them up. It ain't a great plan, but if we can catch Randall's outfit red-handed it'll have bin worth it.'

Ginny came round with a bottle of red eye.

The following morning Harry Tunstall rode out to the Rolling R ranch and spoke to Randall.

'I figured Starret would cause us some trouble,'

Randall said, over a glass of red eye. 'So he's gonna have some men waitin' around an' some other fellas to follow us back here?'

'Dead right,' Tunstall said.

'Well, git back to yer place an' let me know what's goin' on,' Randall said.

'Sure thing,' Tunstall said, finishing his red eye.

A short while later Randall rode down to the cabin that Clanton was using.

'It's that damn Starret,' he said to Clanton. 'You should've got rid of him the first time.'

'Looks like I'm gonna have to look after him agin,' Clanton said. 'I'll git him this time.'

'See that you do,' Randall said.

Randall went to the door of the ranch house and called for Mahon.

'Yeah, boss?' the red-haired hand said to him.

'How would you an' the boys like to go into town tonight? All drinks are on me,' Randall said to him. 'Roust the place up. Don't kill anybody, but let them know you've bin there.'

'Sure, boss, any special occasion?'

Randall laughed. 'Just enjoy yerselves.'

That night Starret and some of the boys from Longstreet's ranch rode out along the trail looking for any signs of the barn-burners. There were none.

'How did things go?' Ginny asked Starret when they got back.

117

'Pretty quiet. It was a lot to hope for if them barn-burners came out on our first night,' he said, digging into his ham and eggs.

'You gonna do the same tonight?' Ginny asked him.

'Sure, but first off I gotta go into Lonesome an' see if everythin's OK there,' he told her.

Half an hour later he took the trail to Lonesome.

His first stop was at the Fair Lady. Harold was sweeping out the place.

'Things OK?' he asked Harold.

'We did a heap of trade last night. Could have used you round here,' Harold said leaning on his broom.

'Things got a bit wild?' Starret asked him.

Harold hesitated for a moment. 'Not exactly. We had most of the crew from the Rolling R in here last night. An' that's unusual. They don't usually come in until the end of the month to spend their wages, but last night it was like they'd bin paid double. Damn near drank the place dry an' wrecked it.'

Starret frowned. 'I don't like the sound of this,' he said to Harold.

'Gave Cheryl an' Shirley a bad time. Didn't exactly hurt them but it got a bit rough.'

'Any damage?' Starret asked him.

'Some,' Harold said.

'Make out a bill. I'll give it to Randall when I get up there,' Starret said.

The stage was just pulling out when Starret got to his office. The town bum was hanging around the office with a letter in his hand.

'Stage guard asked me to give you this. Said the letter was from Fairfax about Anderson. Said you'd fix me up with some money fer a drink.'

Starret took a dollar out of his pocket and gave it to the bum. Taking the envelope, he was about to go into his office when a thought struck him.

'Come back here,' he told the bum.

'It was them Rollin' R boys that did the damage last night,' the bum said quickly to Starret.

Starret unlocked the office door. 'It ain't about that,' Starret told him.

The bum followed him in. Starret closed the door behind him and sat down opposite the bum.

'Do you know Fred Durkin?' he asked the bum.

'Sure I know Fred Durkin – we used to drink together when we had the money,' the bum said nervously.

'That's what I wanted to talk to you about,' Starret said putting another coin on the desk.

The bum's eyes lit up and his tongue ran over his lips. 'What do you want to know?'

'It's about his wife's brother strikin' gold,' Starret said.

The bum started to laugh then cut it short. 'Her brother never struck gold. He died on the way to the California gold fields,' the bum said.

119

'So when did Durkin quit drinkin'?' Starret asked the bum.

'About the time—' he stopped again.

'About the time we got arrested?' Starret said.

'Yeah,' the bum said. 'If it's money an' Rebecca you're talkin' about. Her ol' man Jasper gave her a heap. An' some folks reckon he gave her a heap just before she married Fred. I think he still lives in the house. Doesn't git out much.'

'Thanks,' Starret told him, tossing him the price of another drink.

He made himself another cup of coffee and sat down to drink it. Starret felt that he was getting near the truth.

FOURTEEN

Harold was still cleaning the place up when Starret went back there.

'You got the bill fer Randall?' he asked Harold.

'Yeah. I got it here,' Harold replied taking an envelope from his vest pocket.

Starret took the bill from the envelope and looked at it.

'I'll git down there to see Randall about this.'

Mahon saw him coming from the porch and went inside the house.

'Starret's comin' this way,' he said to Randall.

Randall grinned wolfishly. 'Good. All we need now is fer Clanton to plug him when he rides out.'

Starret hitched his horse to the rail and went inside.

'Nice to see you, Sheriff,' Randall said affably when he saw Starret.

'Hope you feel that way when you've seen this,' Starret said, dropping the bill on Randall's desk.

Randall read the bill and put it down on the desk. 'The trouble with you, Starret,' he said in a silky voice, 'is that you've bin in the pen for so long you forgot how hard ranch hands work. If you ever knew.'

It took Starret a whole lot not to drag Randall across the desk.

'You ain't lookin' so good, Sheriff,' Mahon said.

'Just be sure you pay fer the damage,' Starret said to Randall.

'Anythin' you say, Sheriff,' Randall said smugly.

Starret said nothing. He turned and walked out of the ranch house.

He saw half a dozen of the ranch hands standing outside the bunkhouse.

Clanton was in a thicket a couple of miles away from Randall's ranch, his Winchester across his knees. The clear air enabled him to see Starret coming from a fair distance away. He took a few steps back into the thicket and raised the Winchester.

Some way out, Starret caught sight of the sun on a metal part of the Winchester. He braced himself for the shot.

When it came, he flung himself out of the saddle, rolled over then lay still on the ground.

Slowly, Clanton got to his feet and looked towards the trail where Starret lay. There was no movement.

Cautiously, he started down there, carelessly trailing the Winchester behind him.

Starret heard a squelch as Clanton came through the mud. He waited until Clanton's body was over him. He was near enough. Starret rolled towards Clanton, mud clinging to him, and sweeping Clanton's legs from under him. Clanton fell on top of him, losing his grip on the Winchester.

They both scrambled up and Clanton grabbed Starret's shirt from the front and tried to pull Starret to his knees, but Starret braced his body, took a step backwards and punched the off-balance Clanton in the face. He felt the warm blood on his hands. Clanton broke free, blood streaming down his face. Despite the blood and pain Clanton reached behind him and drew a Bowie knife from the sheath.

Starret drew his .45 and levelled it at Clanton. 'Drop the knife,' Starret shouted.

Clanton kept coming. Starret shot him through the heart. Clanton's legs buckled and he went down.

The rain had started again and was beating against Starret's face as he looked at Clanton's body in the mud. Somewhere behind the thicket Clanton's horse whinnied.

Starret holstered his smoking gun and walked up the hill. Taking the horse by the reins he led it to Clanton's lifeless body and threw the corpse over the saddle. He got mounted and headed for Lonesome, leading Clanton's horse by the reins.

Longstreet met him coming into Lonesome. 'Who've you got there, Sheriff?' he asked Starret as he got to his office.

Starret climbed down and hitched his horse to the rail. 'Doc Clanton. That's the name you knew him by. I ran into him in the pen. He answered to the name of Dawlish. He was a killer fer hire,' Starret said, handing the reins of Clanton's horse to Longstreet. 'Do me a favour, take this horse down to Al at the livery. Then come back here.'

'Sure thing, Sheriff,' Longstreet said taking the reins from Starret.

Starret unlocked the office and went inside. After a while Longstreet came back.

'Git the boys ready fer tonight. I reckon them barn-burners will be out lookin' fer mischief.'

'Anythin' you say, Sheriff,' Longstreet said and went off to spread the word.

Harry Tunstall rode on to the Rolling R spread as it was getting towards early evening.

'Got some bad news fer you, Randall,' he said. 'Longstreet came over. Starret's shot Clanton.'

Randall looked at him. 'Damn Jim Starret,' he said.

'They're goin' out agin tonight, he ain't gonna give up.'

Randall thought for a minute. 'Here's what we do, I'll take half the boys an' make it look as if we're headin' fer the Halton place. Then an hour after we've gone, Mahon can take the rest of the boys an' burn the Henley place. Maybe toss in some dynamite.'

'OK,' Tunstall said. 'I'd best be gettin' back.'

Randall sent for Mahon and told him how it was going to be. 'An' take Fallon along. He might as well earn his keep.'

'I'll get some dynamite,' Mahon said.

When they were ready Randall and his men met up outside the ranch house and headed in the direction of the Halton place. An hour later Mahon rode out in the direction of the Henley ranch.

Dave Henley was out with some of his hands and some of the other ranchers looking for the barn-burners.

Mahon got down from his saddle and crept along the path near Henley's ranch house.

He cat-footed back. 'Everything's OK.' He got mounted and lit the fuse to the dynamite.

He spurred his horse and led the charge down the trail. As he neared the ranch house he drew back his arm and tossed the stick of dynamite at the house.

It curved though the air, the fuse spluttering. Behind him Mahon could hear his men shooting at Henley's hands as they stumbled half-asleep out of the bunkhouse.

As Mahon peeled off from the rest of his men the dynamite exploded. The ranch house was ripped apart and tossed in all directions. Henley's two kids were blown to bits along with Henley's wife.

Mahon spurred his horse and guided it back to where his men had finished shooting up the ranch hands.

'That's it, boys. Let's git back to Rolling R land.'

Randall was waiting for them when they got there. 'No trouble?' he asked Mahon.

'No. No trouble,' Mahon said, grinning.

Dave Henley and the rest of his boys got back to his ranch just after first light. The first thing they saw were the bodies of the ranch hands that Mahon and his men had shot down. For a second Henley couldn't believe it. Some yards away was the remains of his ranch house; he guessed what had happened to his family. His face became purple with rage. One of the hands who had ridden out with him grabbed the reins of his horse and held them fast.

'We know who did this, Dave, but you'll make things worse if you go after Randall on yer own. You'll only git yerself killed to no purpose.'

'Take it easy, boss,' another hand said.

'I'll take it easy,' Henley said, 'just as soon as I git some lead into Randall.'

He suddenly dragged his horse's head round and spurred it hard. The horse took off with Henley holding his Winchester.

One of his hands lit out after him. 'Git word to Starret. He'll be up near the Halton place,' the hand yelled over his shoulder.

Two of the hands galloped out of the yard and up towards the Halton place.

A fire of fury had been started in Henley. It blazed more fiercely the nearer he got to Randall's ranch.

'Hold it, Henley,' a voice yelled as he got to the boundary.

'Just where the hell d'you think you're goin'?' Mahon called out to him.

Henley hauled on the reins. He looked across at Mahon who was coming out of some trees with his .45 in his hand.

'I'm goin' to see yer boss about what's bin happening' at my ranch.'

Henley hesitated. Mahon didn't. He shot Henley out of the saddle.

Mahon was feeling pretty pleased with himself. He got down to help himself to Henley's new Winchester when a piece of lead dug into the ground between his legs.

He turned quickly and found himself looking down the barrel of Starret's .45.

'Unfasten yer rig,' Starret said quietly to him. 'Then get in yer saddle.'

Mahon moved slowly as Starret watched him.

'You're doin' fine,' Starret told him.

When the rig had fallen into the mud, Starret said, 'Git in yer saddle.'

Mahon mounted slowly. 'I'm takin' you in fer

murder,' Starret told him. 'Unless you want to make a deal, an' tell me how I can get my hands on Randall.'

'Not a hope, Sheriff. I won't hang. Randall will get me out,' Mahon said confidently to Starret as they headed for Lonesome. They rode through the streets as dawn was breaking.

'How long do you reckon you can hold me?' Mahon asked Starret, as Starret locked him in a cell.

'As long as I have to,' Starret told him, as he walked back to his office.

Starret settled in his chair behind his desk. A couple of hours later Randall came in with a couple of his hands from his ranch.

'Where's my foreman?' Randall demanded of Starret.

'In a cell where he belongs an' where he's stayin' until I can get a judge to try him fer murder,' Starret said, watching Randall's men closely.

'On whose say so?' Randall snapped.

'Mine,' Starret said rising from his chair.

Randall's men backed away as Starret stood up.

'We'll see,' Randall said.

Starret watched him go while wondering what his next move would be.

'You got any of that dynamite left?' Randall asked Grogan when they got back to the ranch.

'Sure,' he was told. 'You goin' visitin' Mahon?'

'Yeah. Make me up somethin' special that'll just blow Mahon up an' not the whole jail,' Randall said with a macabre grin. Just before nightfall Randall met his hands outside the ranch house.

'You fellers go make some noise at the Fair Lady, like you did the other night. I'll blow up Mahon's cell. An' remember I was in there with you all the time,' Randall said.

'Reckon that'll do the job,' Grogan said.

The horsemen headed up the trail to Lonesome.

It was just getting dark when Randall held up his hand. 'You boys git to the Fair Lady. I'll go blow up Mahon.' He pulled off the trail and watched them head to town. When they disappeared he rode into Lonesome by a roundabout way.

Everywhere was quiet. It was like the first day that Starret got there. Randall rode up the back streets. He cut round the back of the jail. He felt his way along until he came to Mahon's cell. Taking two sticks of the dynamite from his pocket, he lit the fuse and dropped them into the cell. Randall ran for his horse. He scrambled into the saddle as the dynamite exploded.

Starret had to go to the Fair Lady when one of Harold's boys came in. 'Can you git down to the saloon? Randall's boys are goin' crazy agin.'

Starret scrambled to his feet and followed the man down to the Fair Lady.

He heard the shooting and the hurrahing halfway

down the block. He drew his gun and pushed his way through the batwings. The first thing he saw was a couple of Randall's boys manhandling Cheryl. He fired two shots into the ceiling.

'Hold it,' he shouted at the top of his voice. 'You fellers make a habit of this?'

Just then the dynamite that had been thrown into Mahon's cell exploded.

Starret dropped his six-gun into the leather and ran out of the saloon cursing himself. He heard a sarcastic cheer come from the saloon.

FIFTEEN

At the end of the street leading to his office, Starret
stopped and watched a column of smoke rising into
the night. He turned and ran back towards the
saloon.

He pushed in through the batwing doors. Randall
was leaning on the bar, drinking a beer.

'Lost somebody, Starret?' he sneered.

Starret felt like grabbing Randall and beating the
hell out of him.

Starret knew there was nothing he could do.
Nobody in the place was going to go up against
Randall. He looked at Cheryl, but she avoided
looking at him.

Starret turned and walked out of the saloon. In the
street he came across Longstreet and his men from
the ranch.

'Not a sign of anybody tonight,' Longstreet said.

'No. They're all in the Fair Lady,' Starret answered

131

him. 'I'm headin' back to see what's left of my office,' and he started walking that way.

The piece of lead passed within an inch of his head. Starret flung himself into the mud. Longstreet's boys got off their horses right quick.

Another piece of lead buried itself in the mud by Starret's head. Drawing his six-gun Starret fired in the direction of the flash he had seen coming from the alley.

There was a yell. Starret got to his feet, followed by Longstreet's men; they headed for the alley.

'Whoever it was is long gone,' Longstreet said.

Starret looked round the alley. 'Maybe not,' he said.

Longstreet and the hands from his ranch followed him down the alley.

'Somebody's lying in the mud,' Starret called to the men behind him. He stopped when he came to the body. He and Longstreet bent down and turned the body over. 'Jasper Stone,' Starret said. 'Give me a hand gettin' him down to Rebecca's house,' he told the others.

They carried the man's body down to Rebecca's house.

'We ain't gotta key,' Starret said, 'an' the house is in darkness. Break the door down.'

Two of the men did so. Starret and Longstreet carried Jasper inside.

'Git a couple of lamps lit,' Starret said.

Somebody got a lamp lit. Jasper Stone was laid on the carpet in the back room of the house.

'He ain't got much time,' Longstreet said.

'Find Fred and Rebecca an' git them in here,' Starret said.

There was a noise on the stairs and the door was pushed open. Fred and Rebecca, still looking half-asleep, came in.

Rebecca bent down to look at her pa.

'Why did he do it, Rebecca?' Starret asked her.

'He gave me the money to buy the shop fer me an' Fred. Then he heard us talkin' about you comin' back an' he got out without us knowing an' took a couple of shots at you.'

'That was when Fallon saw you an' Fred near the general store?' Starret asked, 'We've sent fer a doc, but it's too late,' he told them.

Starret watched Stone for a minute. 'I'm goin' over to see Fletcher,' he said to Longstreet.

It took him a while to get an answer from Fletcher's house, but in the end old man Fletcher opened the door with a lamp in his hand.

Starret didn't wait. He pushed his way in. 'Jasper Stone's dead. Rebecca told us everythin'. Tell me what you know,' Starret said impatiently.

'She came to me about Fred. Somehow he'd found out about the extra money in the bank,' Fletcher said shakily. 'Fred wasn't always a drunk. He's had some good jobs. He used to work fer Wells

Fargo. Anyway, he ran across one of his old buddies. Him an' Fred got talkin', an' he told Fred about the extra money comin' into the bank. Fred and Rebecca were desperate fer money. Rebecca came to see me about it, an' we fixed up to steal it. It was easy to git into the bank. The only thing is he had nobody to blame. Lucky fer us, you boys came along.'

Starret grabbed Fletcher round the throat and shook him. Then said, 'Go on.'

'We knew you'd be swimmin' with the weather bein' so hot.'

'So you tipped Dempster off.'

'Yeah, we tipped Dempster off.'

Starret swore long and hard at the old man.

'There ain't much more I can say,' Fletcher said.

'There's a couple of things you can say,' Starret said to him. 'Where did the money go?'

'Cheryl's pa had some. Sent a couple of orphans to college back East with it.'

'Dempster, what did he have to do with it.'

'Dempster did one stupid thing. He shot a prisoner in the back. Told folks he'd tried to make a run fer it. Guess that's when he figured he was too old to carry the badge. Randall found out about it. An' it was Randall that fixed it so Fallon got the job.'

'That it?' Starret asked him.

'Yeah.'

Starret looked at the old man. Now he had it all. Except for Randall.

*

Starret made up his mind. Fletcher was sitting quietly in the chair. He walked quickly over to Rebecca Durkin's shop. Longstreet and his boys were still there.

'I've got the whole thing out of Fletcher. All we got to do is go over to the Fair Lady and arrest them. The whole crew's in there along with some innocent folks, so if there's gonna be some shootin', I don't want the whole thing turning into a bloodbath.'

There was a murmur of assent.

'How are we gonna git them folks out?' Longstreet said.

'We could git Randall's crew out pretty easy,' Longstreet's boy Ethan said.

Everybody looked at him.

'Let's hear it,' Starret said.

'They've bin in there a while now,' he went on. 'If they're still drinkin' they must be nearly unconscious by now.'

'They might be,' Starret said thoughtfully.

'I'll go down there an' see. You come down right after me,' Ethan said.

'It's worth tryin',' old man Longstreet said.

'You git down there,' Starret said to Ethan. 'I'll git the men outside, an' they can git in there right off.'

Starret got his men outside as soon as Ethan Longstreet was ready He went along the street down to the Fair Lady.

135

Inside the Fair Lady the crew of the Rolling R were pretty drunk. Most of them were unconscious lying face down at the tables. Randall was snoring at a table next to the honky-tonk piano. Harold had gone upstairs out of the way. Cheryl and Shelia were looking pretty bored at the one of the tables.

'Looks like we saved ourselves some trouble,' Ethan Longstreet said to Cheryl. 'We're gonna git them outside. I'll git the sheriff.'

Starret and the others came in and started to take the guns off the drunken cowhands. Then they took them down to the jail and locked them up. It was pretty crowded because one of the cells – where Mahon had been – was a wreck.

Randall and most of his crew woke up just after sunlight. For a while he and his crew kicked up a ruckus in their cells.

Starret came in with a couple of men he had deputized. He was toting a shotgun. 'Quit the ruckus,' he told Randall's men.

'What d'you think yer doin'?' Randall yelled, his head thumping.

'Holdin' you an' yer boys fer murder an' barn-burnin',' Starret told him.

'I hope you can prove it,' Randall blustered.

'I can prove it,' Starret told him. 'I moved Mahon out some place safe in case you tried somethin'.'

Randall grabbed the cell bars and shook them with rage.

'Behave yerself,' Starret told him, 'or I'll charge you with damagin' public property.' He and his deputies went back to the office.

Randall calmed down enough to think straight. If he hoped to avoid swinging he'd have to find out where Mahon was and get to him. He wondered if Mahon knew about Clanton's book. That would hang him for sure.

Starret came back an hour later with some coffee. 'Just to prove I ain't all bad,' he said sarcastically. 'I'm gonna have to let some of your boys outta here. I ain't got proof to hold you all.' He pushed the mugs through the bars and left them to drink the coffee.

'I've bin good to you fellers,' Randall said quietly after Starret had gone. A couple of them looked at him. 'If you get outta here, here's what I want you to do. Find out where Mahon is an' get word back here. Leave the rest to me.'

The morning wore on and Starret came back. 'Dixon, Simpson, you're out,' he said, unlocking the door. 'Collect yer irons from the office. Then git outta town, an' stay out.'

Dixon and Simpson went up to the office and collected their irons.

'Where d'you reckon they've got that bastard, Mahon, stashed?' Simpson asked his buddy.

'Dunno, but we'd better get him found,' Dixon said when they got outside.

'There's one of them fellers that took us to the jail

last night,' Simpson said to his *amigo*. 'Maybe we could ask him.'

They followed old man Longstreet into the alley next to Al's.

'There's only one ol' man in there,' Dixon said as they followed Longstreet into the alley.

Longstreet knocked on the livery door. Al pushed it open. The two men bundled him into the livery.

Simpson pushed the door closed.

'Keep quiet, both of you,' Dixon snarled after he had pulled out his six-gun.

Simpson grabbed Longstreet by the throat and pushed his gun under Longstreet's chin. 'Where's Mahon? Where have you got him stashed?' he demanded.

Longstreet shook his head, but Simpson pistol-whipped him.

He raised his hands to do it again, but Dixon caught him by the wrist. 'That's a waste of time,' he said and drew his own gun.

Dixon grabbed Al and cocked the gun after he had pushed it against Al's temple. 'Where's Mahon?' he asked Longstreet. 'It looks like yer buddy's gonna git it.'

Longstreet looked at Al. 'Up at the Halton place.'

'That wasn't too hard was it?' Dixon pulled the trigger.

He tossed a look at Simpson. Simpson shot Longstreet.

The two gunmen rode out of Lonesome and took the trail up to the Halton place.

They stopped at the gate, dismounted and cat-footed through the foliage until they came in sight of the ranch house.

'Seems quiet enough,' Dixon said to his sidekick. 'Them Haltons must still be in town. I saw them before we shot them other two fellers at the livery.'

They moved towards the ranch house.

Dixon eased the latch up and looked inside. 'He's here.'

Simpson followed him in. Mahon was tied to a chair, a gag in his mouth.

'Hi,' Dixon said good-naturedly as Mahon was starting to look worried. He pulled the gag out of Mahon's mouth. 'The boss wants us to take you back. I think he's heard some talk about you doin' a deal with Starret.'

'It ain't like that,' Mahon said quickly.

'Fine,' Simpson said. 'You tell him what it's like.' He started to push the gag back into Mahon's mouth.

He and Dixon loosened the ropes round Mahon. They dragged him outside and wrestled him on to his horse. They rode hard to get to the Rolling R spread.

Randall was working on a plan to get out of jail. Another problem had hit him. Clanton's book. He'd have to get out of jail and get his hands on that book.

One of his men was left in the cell. 'You wanna help me get out of here?' Randall asked him.

'Sure,' Mason said.

'You got any lucifers?' Randall asked him.

'Yeah,' Mason said, hauling a box out of his vest pocket.

'Git one lit then holler fer some help,' Randall told him, picking up an empty tin mug from the floor.

'That'll cause more trouble,' Mason said. 'There's a heap of deputies down there.'

'There's just Longstreet's boy. All them other deputies have bin sent back to their ranches. Starret's gone to the eats place to get himself some grub. He reckons he's done with us.'

Mason had got a smoky fire going by putting a lucifer to his pillow which was filled with straw.

'Start hollerin' an' keep it loud,' Randall said standing by the wall.

Mason kept hollering until Ethan came into the corridor.

'What's the noise about?' he yelled, as smoke began to fill the cell.

'We're gonna fry or burn unless you git us outta here,' Mason said coughing and holding his chest.

The smoke had covered Randall, who was keeping quiet.

'Git us outta here,' Mason yelled again.

Ethan took his keys from his belt and unlocked the

140

cell door. Straightaway, he began to cough. Randall hit him over the head with the tin mug.

Longstreet went down. Randall grabbed his six-gun out of its holster.

He picked up the deputy's keys and followed Mason out. He locked the cell and tossed the keys in there.

'Let's git,' he said to Mason.

They dashed up the corridor to the empty office. Randall grabbed his rig and Mason did the same.

'Hold on,' Randall said. He opened the door and looked outside. 'It's clear,' he said to Mason. They both went out into the deserted street.

'Let's head fer the livery an' git our horses,' Randall said, looking over his shoulder.

They went off that way. 'Looks like somebody got here before us,' Mason said, treading over the two bodies in the livery stable.

'Git saddled and mounted,' Randall said sarcastically. 'We'll come back an' bury them later.'

They saddled up their horses and galloped down the alley.

Starret saw them as he was coming out of the eats place. It took him a second to work out what had happened. He raced over to the jail.

SIXTEEN

'Nice to see you agin,' Randall said to Mahon, who was still tied up. 'Bin hearin' some bad things about you. Real bad things.'

'It wasn't like that,' Mahon said.

'Yeah, that's what you told us,' Simpson said filling up a glass with red eye and handing it to Randall.

Randall tossed the drink back. 'Let's hear your side of it.'

Mahon had gone pale. 'Starret had me over a barrel. I had to talk, but I figured you'd get me out,' Mahon said. His mouth was dry.

'We got you out,' Randall smiled.

'Yeah, thanks boss,' Mahon said.

'Well,' Randall said. 'You ain't over a barrel any more.'

Mahon looked relieved.

Randall poured himself another glass of red eye.

He drank slowly. 'You two have done some real good work. Pour yerselves a drink, then find a real strong rope and a real quiet place an' hang him up there.'

Silvio and Ginny had just got back to Lonesome. They saw Starret running for the jail.

'What happened?' Silvio asked Starret from the porch.

'I ain't bin in there yet, but I saw Randall an' Mason headin' off some place in a real hurry.'

They went inside after him. The smoke was just drifting into the office.

Starret ran to the cells with the others just after him. He swore as he pulled at the cell door. Randall had locked it and tossed the key inside.

'Stand back,' Starret shouted. He drew his six-gun and shot the lock off. He went to get Ethan. He picked up the keys and tossed them over to Silvio. 'Let them other fells out, but make sure you got them covered.'

Starret got his arm round Ethan's shoulder and started to carry him out of the cell. The other prisoners were getting anxious about getting out.

Silvio and Ginny got them out on to the veranda, their hands above their heads and looking miserable as it started to rain once more.

'How are you feelin'?' Starret asked Ethan in the eats place where he had taken him to get the smoke out of his lungs.

'Not too bad,' was the answer.

'Some coffee an' somethin' to eat, over here,' Starret shouted over to a waitress.

The street was filling up with curious folks when news of the fire in the jail had got round. Starret reckoned that some of the folks had come to see the barn-burners get some of their own medicine.

'Git a couple of deputies,' he said to Silvio, 'an' we'll git after Randall an' the other feller. Git some of the posse. They're in the eats place.'

Silvio pushed his rifle into a bystander's hands. 'Consider yerself deputized.'

'Hold it.' Starret said. He had been talking to some *hombre* who had come up from the livery.

'What is it?' Silvio asked as he came hurrying over to the hitch rail.

'Longstreet an' Al have bin shot down at the livery,' Starret told him.

'Let's get goin' before they git too far away,' Silvio said, climbing into the saddle.

'Let's ride,' Starret said, mounting up.

Ginny watched them go, feeling sick as Starret disappeared from sight.

Simpson and Dixon had Mahon tied to his saddle as they rode away from the Rolling R spread.

Dixon had a swig of red eye from a bottle he had filched from Randall as they went to get Mahon in the saddle. He handed it to Simpson. Simpson took a swig and handed it back.

'Sorry about the way things turned out, Mahon, but me an' Simpson won't keep you hanging around fer too long.' Simpson and Dixon laughed so hard they nearly fell out of their saddles. They were still laughing when they collided with the posse.

'Somethin's sure makin' you fellers laugh,' Starret said as he and some more members of the posse levelled their guns at Dixon and Simpson.

'Glad to see you, Sheriff,' Mahon shouted from the rear. 'These rats were gonna hang me.'

'Glad we got here in time then,' Starret shouted back to him. 'Keep yer eyes on these fellers. OK, you two, where's Randall?'

The two men looked at each other.

'Don't waste my time. You got one rope. We might use it to stretch two necks.'

Dixon and Simpson looked uneasily at each other again.

'You do that, Sheriff,' Mahon shouted encouragingly.

'Get that rope,' Starret shouted to one of the posse.

'OK, what do you want to know,' Dixon said.

'Everythin',' Starret told him.

'Randall is back at the Rollin' R,' Dixon said. 'He'll be waitin' fer you.'

'Fergit the rope fer the time bein',' Starret said.

'Silvio an' some of you fellers make sure Mahon an' these other two get back to jail. The rest of you, follow me.'

SEVENTEEN

They headed for the Rolling R spread. Starret watched the trail up ahead for any signs of an ambush.

They rode on to the spread with no trouble.

Starret got some of the posse to wait among some trees. The other half he sent round the back to wait for the shooting to start.

'I'm gonna give them a chance to give themselves up,' Starret said.

Leaving the cover of the trees he approached the ranch house.

'That's close enough,' Randall shouted from the house as he sent a piece of lead digging into the ground between Starret's legs.

'You're cornered,' Starret said. 'Come out an' I'll see you git a fair trial. The same goes fer yer buddies.'

'Save it, Starret,' Randall called back. 'We'll stay here till hell freezes over before we come out.'

'Don't be stupid, Randall,' Starret called back. 'You're finished.'

Randall fired two more pieces of lead into the ground where Starret was standing.

'I can take a hint,' Starret said, as he started back.

'They're gonna make a fight of it,' he told the posse.

The rain had stopped and a watery sun had come up.

'When I give the word, fire a few shots to let them know we're serious an' let them fellers round the back know we've got started.'

A couple of minutes passed and Starret said, 'All right, now.' A ragged volley of shots came from the cover of the trees.

'We're gonna have to git nearer,' Starret said, after an hour of shooting. 'You two boys get in that barn, an' git up as high as you can.'

Two of the posse ran for the barn and almost made it. One of them took a piece of lead in the shoulder and went down screaming. The other member of the posse kept on running until he got to the barn.

'We can't just leave him out there screamin' like that,' one of his buddies shouted.

'I'll go an' git him in the barn,' Starret said, laying his rifle on the ground. 'Cover me.' Starret ran for it, the posse keeping down the fire from the inside of the ranch house.

Starret got the man over his shoulder and ran into

the barn with him.

'You all right?' a voice came from the loft.

'Yeah. I got him. What can you see from up there?' Starret shouted back.

'Some kinda pow-wow goin' on. Can't see much else though.'

'I'll come up an' have a look as soon as I've taken a look at Richards.'

Richards was unconscious, his face white and drawn, his breathing noisy and shallow. Starret took off his bandanna and wiped Richards's face with it. He looked round until he saw a couple of canteens hanging on a post. He went over and shook them. They were full.

Quickly, he took one over to where Richards was lying. Richards opened his eyes.

'How are y'feelin'?' Starret asked him.

'Not too great, Jim,' Richards said, as though it cost him a lot.

'We'll get you out as soon as we can,' Starret told him, putting a canteen to his lips. 'I'll be back.'

Starret climbed the ladder that led into the loft. 'Anythin' happenin', Williams?'

Sam Williams shook his head. 'They've stopped talkin'. It looks like they're just waitin'.'

Starret moved to the edge of the loft and looked into the sky. Soon it would be dark.

'Sam, keep yer eyes open an' cover me. I want to see what the posse's doin'.' He climbed down the

149

ladder and went to where Richards was lying.

'How are y'feelin'?' he asked Richards again.

'Not so great,' Richards mumbled.

'Just hang on. Everythin's gonna be all right.'

Starret moved to the door of the barn and looked outside, then gave a wave hoping that the posse would understand it.

He braced himself and ran for it. As he ran he heard a couple of shots. Then a couple of posse men on the edge of the wood started giving him some covering fire.

More shots came in his direction and then Starret was in the cover of the wood. He leaned against a tree getting his breath back.

Suddenly he heard a sharp crack and the earth shuddered and shook. There was a long rumble of falling timber, followed by the intense crackle of flames as the fire after the explosion took hold. He went back to the edge of the wood. The barn was a smouldering ruin.

'Them bastards,' one of the posse shouted. There was an outbreak of firing from the posse.

'Stop that,' Starret called out. The firing died away.

He looked again at where the barn had stood. It reminded him of the Carson place. He thought that he wouldn't have to be going back for Richards or Williams. The thought made him angry.

'Hamilton, git round the back to where them

150

other fellers are an' see how things are back there.'

'Gotcha, Jim,' Hamilton called back. Starret heard Hamilton move through the woods. A few minutes later he heard him gallop away. Starret walked round his men to see how they were holding on. Most of them sounded OK and a couple were itching to get at Randall and those in the ranch house. Starret walked to the edge of the wood and rolled a stogie. He scratched a lucifer and touched the stogie with it. Somebody grabbed him by the shoulder and dragged him back into the cover of the trees.

'Best take a bit more care with them lucifers now it's gettin' dark,' Hardaker, the blacksmith, told him.

'Thanks, Hardaker,' Starret replied. Then something occurred to Starret. 'Git the men together. Randall an' his men might try to git out while it's dark.'

'Anythin' you say, Jim.' Hardaker went to see the men.

He got back a few minutes later. 'I told them. One or two of the boys reckon Randall has got the horses corralled at the back of the house, near the stable.'

Starret groaned inwardly. He had forgotten about the corral at the back of the house.

'Maybe we could rush them,' Hardaker said.

Starret thought for minute. 'OK. There are enough of us. Git everybody ready. We'll just have to hope that our men round the back will cotton on to what we're doin' an' give us a hand.'

Starret checked his six-gun. 'C'mon boys. Start out slow an' quiet.' His half of the posse moved out along the front stretch of the wood. The temperature was starting to go up. Starret walked head up, senses alert. The house loomed in the dark. There were no lights anywhere. The whole thing had an eerie quality to it. As he got level with the wreck of the front barn some wood crackled and looked as if it was going to flare up again.

Starret braced himself expecting a shot. The posse was halfway between the wreck of the barn and the house when the front door opened. Starret had a brief glimpse of a figure, its arm drawn back ready to throw something.

He realized in a second what it was. 'Get down,' he yelled. He hit the wet ground. The rest of the posse went down a second later.

Starret sent a piece of lead in the direction of the front door. He was too late.

Something flew through the evening air. The door was slammed shut and a second later the earth bucked under the explosion, lifting Starret clear of the ground and dumping him right back there. The whole thing stunned Starret. The door opened again and another stick of dynamite was tossed out of the house.

The explosion shook Starret and the posse again.

Before Starret could do anything, the posse was running back to the wood. There was cheering from the inside of the house.

'Anybody hurt?' Starret asked Hardaker.

'Ol' man Jackson. That last stick blew him in two.'

The rest of the posse was shaken. 'I'll git round the other side to see how things are there,' Hardaker said.

'I don't think there were any explosions back there,' Starret said.

Hardaker rode his horse as silently as he could through the trees, till he reached the copse out of range of the ranch house where he found the rest of the posse huddled round a campfire.

'Who's there?' the voice was shaky and frightened.

'Take it easy, Ross. It's me, Hardaker.' He walked into the light given off by the campfire.

'Was that what we figured it was?' Ross asked Hardaker.

'If you mean was it dynamite. Sure it was,' Hardaker said, looking at the faces of the posse round the fire. They would be staying put, he figured.

'It's damned quiet out there,' Randall said to his new foreman, Grogan. 'They're just sittin' round that campfire like we're all gonna be here till the Fourth of July.'

'We've still got enough to shake them up a mite,' Grogan said.

'I've got somethin' else in mind,' Randall told

him. 'There's some horses in the corral about a quarter of a mile down there. Go fetch that dynamite an' we'll git outta here.'

'Anythin' you say, boss,' Grogan said.

Randall watched as Grogan went into the front room. He pulled the curtain up and looked out towards the fire. Things had been OK in this part of the country, but with this Starret carrying the star it was time to move on.

Ten minutes later Grogan came back with the dynamite in his hands.

'Here's what's left,' he said to Randall. There were six sticks left. Randall took three sticks and left Grogan with the other three.

'Take them three an' fix them up with fuses, an' tell the men to start throwing them,' Randall said to Grogan.

Grogan went to give out the dynamite and returned. 'Done it, boss.'

'Git back in there an' make sure everythin's OK.'

Grogan went back to the front where the other hands were.

Randall waited a few minutes.

A few minutes later he heard the crump of an explosion coming from the front of the ranch house. He opened the door and heard the crump of another explosion. He took the bottle of red eye and finished it off as a third explosion rocked the house.

'Time to go,' he said to himself, and lit one of the

remaining sticks of dynamite and tossed it into the room where his men were crouched at the window, rifles at the ready.

'Sleep tight, boys,' he murmured.

He went out through the back door and waited. Stepping off the porch he lit a stick of dynamite and tossed it in the direction of the posse's campfire. Randall waited for everything to quieten down and ran towards the corral. He lit another stick and tossed it towards the burning ranch house. He didn't wait for the explosion, but carried on running towards the corral.

In the corral the horses were pretty spooked. Randall went to the bunkhouse and kicked the door open. He got himself a saddle and a bridle. A minute later he was in the corral calming the horses down. When he got in the saddle he rode towards where Starret and the posse were. He threw in the last stick, hoping to get Starret. Then he headed for Lonesome.

The posse had been watching the house burning after Randall had tossed a stick into the room where his crew and Fallon had been.

Another stick exploded as Randall rode out to Lonesome to collect Clanton's notebook.

Starret picked himself up along with Hardaker and the other men.

'What was that?' Starret yelled, getting to his feet and looking round. 'Everybody OK?'

One by one they answered that they were.

'Damn it,' Hardaker howled rushing to the edge of the wood. There were clumps of earth, a few pieces of the ranch house and one of Fallon's arms had landed near him. The men stopped in their tracks. A couple of the posse who saw Fallon's arm threw up.

'We ain't gonna be able to identify these fellers,' Hamilton said.

'You ain't gonna be able to identify Randall,' Starret said. 'You can bet he wasn't in there.'

EIGHTEEN

Randall was clear of the ranch and heading for Lonesome. On the edge of town, he changed direction and headed for Clanton's place. He knew the notebook was in the house and he figured that some of the money he had paid Clanton might be in there with it. In that notebook were the names of all the people who had used Clanton's services as a killer. A lot of those people would pay to keep their names away from the law. The muddy streets were just beginning to get light when he got there. He headed for Clanton's house passing the Fair Lady. He noticed a light burning inside the saloon.

Randall took a look round then led his horse down to the stable at the back of Clanton's house, he didn't want any nosy neighbours taking an interest. He leaned on the door forcing it inwards. He took a step inside.

It was cold. In a cupboard he found a bottle of red

eye. Pulling the cork, he took a long swallow. The light was getting stronger now. He opened every drawer in the kitchen but he couldn't find the notebook.

Randall swore to himself as he walked up the stairs. In the back bedroom, he found it under a floor board along with a wad of cash. He opened the notebook and read a couple of lines to be sure he had the right notebook. He smiled and put it in his jacket pocket.

Starret figured the only place Randall could be would be Lonesome.

He rode away from the ranch, leaving Hardaker to get the dead bodies moved, and galloped to the town. He rode down to the street and came to the Fair Lady. Harold saw Starret as he was sweeping the Fair Lady out.

'Hey, Starret,' he called.

Starret gigged his horse towards Harold.

'I was brushing the place out, an' I saw Randall heading down that way,' Harold said, pointing in the direction of Clanton's house.

'Thanks,' replied Starret, and rode down the street.

Randall was leading his horse up the path and was feeling pretty pleased with himself.

'Goin' some place?' The voice sent shivers down his spine. He turned to see Starret standing with his hand on his gun.

'You gonna come quietly?' Starret asked him.

'What do you think?' Randall asked him, going for his gun.

Starret beat him to it. Randall was spun round by the force of Starret's lead, his hat flew off and he went down in the mud. He tried to heave himself up and fell back, letting out a last fearful groan.

Starret bent down to check that Randall was dead and found the notebook and cash in his pocket.

'You sure make the heck of lot of a noise in a mornin', Starret,' Cheryl said.

'Sorry if I woke you, but I gotta myself a new pair of boots.' Starret smiled and got into the saddle and went to see Ginny.

LE 07/10